I0640985

Harriet Prescott Spofford

An Inheritance

Harriet Prescott Spofford

An Inheritance

ISBN/EAN: 9783743441781

Manufactured in Europe, USA, Canada, Australia, Japa

Cover: Foto ©Andreas Hilbeck / pixelio.de

Manufactured and distributed by brebook publishing software (www.brebook.com)

Harriet Prescott Spofford

An Inheritance

AN INHERITANCE

I

It is not at all an unpleasant thing to
come into a little property when it is attended by no personal loss.   And there was
really no personal loss, as people said, that
could attend Miss Barbara Camperdoun's
inheritance from a cousin who, it was
thought, had wished a number of years ago
to be something nearer than a cousin, but
had been promptly discouraged by that
worthy lady.   It was not that Miss Barbara, as her sister-in-law once said, had no
idea of marrying anything less than a
prince of the blood royal, and as no prince
was proposing, had therefore remained sin-
gle; but as she herself said, whatever ulti-
mate reason she kept unspoken, she pre-
ferred to be no one in particular in Boston, .

so far as a Camperdoun could be no one in particular, to being the first lady in a mountain village.

Besides, she might not have been first lady, had she gone. The minister's wife—no, a country minister's wife, Miss Barbara assured herself, could hardly take precedence of her, with the minister more or less dependent on her good will. But the doctor's wife—ah! everyone was dependent on the good will of the doctor, that viceroy of life and death; and Dr. Donner was a man of power. She remembered seeing him when breaking a horse for her uncle, a vast black brute of a Bellerophon, while she was a girl visiting at Woodsedge. Someone said that now he was content with horses other people had broken, for driving about the country on his practice that went far and wide among the hills. She had seen him occasionally since then, at her brother's house when he had come down about her cousin's affairs, or about his own, from time to time.

Miss Barbara had gone up to Woodsedge

now, a day and night's journey, to take possession of her house, bringing with her Luisa,
her exceedingly pretty niece. It was at the
close of a long and gay season, through
which Luisa had danced and dined and
lunched, gone to theatre and opera and pri-
vate views and five-o'clock teas and dinner
dances, posed in living pictures and assisted
in skirt-dances given for charity to a femi-
nine audience, and Miss Barbara said the
mountain air would bring Luisa back to
a normal standard of health and morals.
And besides, she was not going alone, anyway!

Luisa was certainly below normal standard now, sleepless by night, and languid
and listless by day, and in danger of losing
that wonderful bloom, softer than the tint
on the petal of the sweetbrier rose, that
flushed the oval of her cheek, and bright-
ened the lustre of the dark eye under its
drooping lid and shadowy lashes, and deepened the red of the tender, pulpy mouth.
Miss Barbara had thought, apropos of her

sister-in-law's speech, and when she looked at Luisa's lithe and slender shape, the abundance of her dark hair, the modelling of every feature, that if royal princes were really in question, here was a girl to be mentioned! But although, of course, that was idle talk, Miss Barbara gave it to be understood that what money she had—and it was not inconsiderable—was going to Luisa Camperdoun, Luisa being the one thing in this world that the imperious lady loved better than—no, no, as well as herself; about as well, at any rate, as her own way.

No; Miss Barbara's fortune was not by any means inconsiderable, as she had said. It had been a fair share of her father's accumulations in the beginning; and she had always lived with her brother, spending but little, saying to people who appealed for charity that she had charities of her own, and telling the children on birthdays and holidays that she was doing better for them in the future than if she gave them gifts now. Of course, all the connection and acquaintance spoke of Barbara's parsimony; and the amount of her savings and well-turned-over investments was put at various large figures.

The only deviation from her quiet way of holding her own was when she saw the charm that Luisa was going to develop. Then she had more expensive masters than the father thought he should afford, paying, however, only the difference in price; and she had taken her a short European journey. When in her nineteenth year Luisa came out, Miss Barbara had supplied her with a half score of bouquets, lest she should not have enough, although, as it happened, she had too many; she had given the girl everything which could adorn her beauty; she had bought Symphony tickets at nameless prices, and a box at the horse-show; and furbishing up her own old gowns, some of which might well have been heirlooms, she had chaperoned her at the opera; had sat out tiresome germans—Mrs. Camperdoun's

delicate health making her unequal to such
fatigues—and had done her best as a dragon
to keep off the youths who danced on a
small capital, and to see that beauty had its
rights.

The youth who gave her the most trouble
was Penny Gower, an attractive but impe-
cunious young artist, who danced so fault-
lessly that it left him with an exhausted air,
as if he would really be quite unable to stand
if he did not lean back upon past genera-
tions, an air that was often found irresisti-
ble.

To tell the truth, the persistency with
which Penrose Gower loitered about her
was one of the reasons that made Miss
Barbara so resolved upon Luisa's going up
into the hill country with her. Penny had
been painting Luisa's portrait — the work
well under way before Miss Barbara knew
of it. And as it had gone so far, and was
supposed to be a labor of love, Miss Barbara, on her well-worn principle of getting
something for nothing, had allowed the

sittings to proceed, herself accompanying Luisa, however, in the place of the maid, or of Helen Reynolds, or other victim of the hour. But the presence of Miss Barbara had brought back the old exhaustion to Penny's manner, and the picture's progress had been too slow for Miss Barbara's impatient habit.

"That young man," she said, "must have the tired feeling you read of in the patent medicine advertisements."

"She has the stony stare of the gorgon, when she puts up her glass," said Penny, as he was walking on the avenue with Luisa. "She simply paralyzes me; I can't have her coming to the studio, don't you know. I shall find the picture turning into a likeness of her."

"Do it!" exclaimed Luisa. "Do it! It will make your fortune! Composite picture of a Boston family! Hereditary traits coming to the top——"

"Well, I didn't suppose you cared," declared Penny. "But I care."

"Pshaw!" said Luisa.

"A man with a heart in his body," said Penny, flicking a pebble out of the way with his stick, as they swept on past the congregated nurses and luxurious babies who monopolize that way, "ought to keep at a distance from you!"

"Then you are all right," said Luisa, gayly.

"You know the only reason I haven't a heart is——"

"Oh, Penny, Penny!" cried Luisa. "Why will you talk of what you know nothing! And didn't you learn in your anatomy class that the heart is a delicate organ and will never endure being bandied about so? It runs a risk of being broken; and then what will it be good for?"

"To dangle at your belt," he said, moodily.

"How you mix metaphors! One would think I carried scalps at my belt!"

"When you are out on the love-path. But——"

" Oh, I forgot to tell you ! I am going away. Going with Aunt Barbara——"

" Going away ! " said Penny, blankly.

" Yes, into the wilderness."

" And the portrait ? "

" Oh, turn it to the wall."

" Luisa ! The lovely thing—why, my whole heart is in it ! "

" There you go again ! Well, let your heart stay in it, and it will be perfectly safe."

" I believe you have no more heart yourself than there is in that picture ! "

" You just said there was a heart in it. Yours, I believe. So you're wrong there, you see. But I'm coming home. At least I suppose I'm coming home," said Luisa, rather ruefully. " When one is in Aunt Barbara's hands one is never sure of anything. She has come into some property up there ; an old family place, and all that. And she will have me go with her—and it's very provoking just now, and that's the truth ! "

" Well, then," said Penny, brightening.

"Well, then. It's Woodsedge. Up back of the mountains, a perfectly lovely place for a painter to recreate." And Luisa's face was the color of a carnation. "Now you'll say I haven't any heart!" she said. "Oh, dear!" pausing a moment at the crossing, bending forward, and looking over to the river, "isn't that Helen and Anne? Yes, it is; they are going down the alley. Oh, the crews are out!"

"I don't care anything about the crews!" exclaimed Penny.

"Good-by, then; I do."

And the naughty coquette was hurrying away through Gloucester Street, a little afraid, a little ashamed, a little amused, and leaving Penny disconsolate—Penny who was madly in love with her color and her out-lines, her eyes and her dimples, and thought he was in love with her; Penny whom she liked very well, whose devotion she liked very well, whom she found it pleasant to keep in evidence, but whom she knew it would never do in the world for her to marry, even if she had wished, which she didn't.   Very few men, to be sure, had such eyes as Penny—black as a gypsy's, and that sometimes seemed to strike sparks.   But then man cannot live on eyes alone, Luisa had said.   He was a handsome fellow, with his dark, smooth skin ; although, to be sure, his nose was large.   But, there, he hadn't a cent ; so what was the use?

She had reached the corner, when she stopped to gather up her skirt and glance over her shoulder.   Penny was standing where she left him, leaning back a little on his stick ; but the girl who had accosted him—those nodding plumes, the chinchilla capes, that bright plaid of the silken skirt-lining blowing out on the wind that eddied all about the wearer — Luisa murmured to herself that she never could imagine what Penny Gower saw to flirt with in that absurd Fanny Fairfield !

So Miss Barbara had come up to Woods-edge, her nerves very much racked by the day and night's travel ; and after resting

another day and night, had proceeded to ex-
plore the house and feel herself in possession
of her new property.

The commercial value of the property here
was, of course, nothing at all to her in com-
parison with its sentimental value.   She went
over the house with Luisa, somewhat to the
disgust of old Martha, who had been undis-
puted mistress, servant, nurse, and friend,
and who now had to learn that there was
but one mistress where Miss Barbara was ;
and she pointed out its family features—the
room where her grandfather was born, the
room where his mother used to sit in state
and receive homage of the lesser people,
their pictures—it was no wonder that Miss
Barbara was an imperious person.   There
was still much of the beautiful French
porcelain about, a couple of hundred years
old, perhaps, that had been brought up into
the wilderness on the backs of men who
knew what a misstep meant, and some of
the antique silver.

"It's a real find," said Miss Barbara.

" To think of Launce eating with a gold spoon up here in the Ultima Thule every day of his silly life, and taking pleasure in it ! "

" They will be lovely for afternoon teas," said Luisa.

" This old Martha must be a very careful person ; perhaps she will do to keep on with some others. I don't know but we shall have to turn the place into a summer mansion, after all, and bring up your father and mother and Bob and the boys. It has every requisite, you see—ancestral quality, numberless rooms, plenty of land—Goodness, what a gardener can make of these grounds !—mountain air — and, bless my soul, what scenery ! " lifting her lorgnon to look out, a little patronizingly, at the great mountains veiled with sunshine and purple that seemed to be offering her their hospitality.

" We can have golf links——"

" If you want. Croquet is good enough for me, though."

"Well, as you never play either, Aunt Barbara——"

"To be sure, the boys will cry havoc and let loose the dogs of war here and get into that old bog," said Miss Barbara, pursuing her own thoughts. "I don't know if I will have them this year, at any rate. You and I can be very comfortable here without them for one summer——"

"The whole summer?" cried Luisa, in dismay.

"The whole summer. You are run down, and need a good rest from dancing and flirting."

"Well, I sha'n't build up if I am bored to death with nothing to do and no one to see."

"You shall have a horse. And here is this great Bursar for protector. I never did like a mastiff before; but he seems to have taken quite a fancy to us. And you can roam the country with him, and be outdoors most of the time."

"I shall simply die!"

" Oh, no.   There's a very good doctor
here, I believe.   Yes, we might do worse.
And we'll try it."

" Aunt Barbara, you look exactly like
that old portrait, the last one in the lower
hall."

" I ? We used to call her the Iron Lady.
She was a grandmother or a great-grand-
mother somewhere."

" That's what it means then—your iron
will.   Wouldn't Penny have a fine time
with these portraits ! "

" Oh !   Penny ! "

" The strange old masks !   It seems as if
we either had more ancestors than other
people—and a queer lot, too—or else that
they had a furious habit of hanging themselves——"

" Luisa ! " said Miss Barbara.   " How you
do let your tongue run away with you ! "

" Why, what earthly harm in hanging
themselves on the wall in gilt frames ? No,
some of them are old carved wood, aren't
they ? Why, what of it ? They never any

of them paid the penalty of their crimes at the rope's end, did they ? "

"I never knew they committed any crimes," said Miss Barbara, coldly. But she was quite white for a few moments. She alone, perhaps, a keeper of traditions, knew who they were in every generation of the Camperdouns that had themselves pulled down the eternal shadows about them, as her young sister Lona had done, with her own hands. She had always tried to keep the whole subject out of her thoughts—it was never spoken of before the children— and her iron will held her in good stead there. She pulled herself together now. " Well, there were a good many of them," she said. " I suppose travelling portrait-painters happened along——"

" The very thing for Penny ! I'll write him how to turn his summer to account ! "

" Oh, let Penny rest ! "

" Aunt Barbara, you are dangerously near slang. Penny could take his brush and turn those ogres, with their eyes looking all ways of a Sunday, into really valuable antiquities. I'm sure that going through the upper halls at midnight here I shall have to run. I shall know the house is haunted. What if a moonbeam suddenly lights up that pale girl whose eyes look as if she were out of her head—they are, anyway——''

'' There, there, Luisa, don't cultivate ridiculous notions ! You will be very proud of these old portraits some day. Yes, the more I see the house and place, the better I think of it all and its possibilities. And as for Penny—there, Luisa, don't let me hear anything more about him. He bored me to death before I left town, and I should like to have one place free from him. Now, you take Bursar and run along. I am going through the papers in Cousin Launce's desks. I mean to do the thing up thoroughly, and know just where I stand, and all about it.''

'' Poor Aunt Barbara ! It's an awful task. Can't I help you ? Let me have some of them——''

"Didn't you hear me say I was going through them myself? What good would it do me to have you read them? Besides, if Launce had not left them here I shouldn't feel as if he were willing I should read them. To be sure, he may have forgotten to destroy them. He—he—was not perfectly well in his last years. However," said Miss Barbara, in a more sprightly manner, "I should have had the freedom of everything if he had had his way. So I sha'n't hesitate. But I know he did not mean you should overlook his papers, at any rate."

"All right, then," said Luisa. "I am sure I don't want to." And she pursed her pretty lips in a whistle that Bursar, suffering from loneliness, bounded to hear, and was off with him into the overrun and long-neglected garden, where the spring was just beginning to pout in leaf and bud of the old primroses and sweetbriers and spice-buds and honeysuckles. "I suppose," said Luisa, touching the long, red sprays of the bare climbing roses half tenderly, "that the women imprisoned here in their lonely lives loved every inch of you. I dare say there was some poor sweet girl —I will trim you now and help you for their sakes. I shall really feel as if I were doing something for them. I must have had, all told, so much gayer a life than they."

And she began to disentangle the stems, and went searching for a trowel to open the earth around their roots, old Martha looking at her askance from the kitchen window. But at that, Bursar wanted a frolic, or perhaps he recognized Brow trotting along after the doctor's gig, for he was over the wall like a ball, and Luisa, running to the gate and throwing it open, rushed almost into the arms of a young girl, into whose face an apple-blossom color had just mounted—a lovely young girl with a sort of ivory fairness on her perfect features, and with eyes like stars in midnight blue, and pale blonde hair in great masses, and a smile like sunshine, as superbly straight and tall a young girl as Botticelli's Flora.

"Oh, I beg your pardon," said Luisa; "I was afraid the dog would run away."

"He has," said the young girl, smiling. "He won't come back to-day. He loves to go with Brow and the doctor. But he's all right. I suppose—I suppose," she said, hesitatingly, and looking at Luisa a little wistfully, "that you are Miss Camperdoun. And I am Mary Swann. My father is the minister, you know. You are working in the garden. Don't you want to let me help you? I am a famous gardener."

"I was going to work in the garden," said Luisa, "and I should have been delighted to have you help me. But now we will sit down on this bench and have Martha bring us some lemonade and sweet cakes. Poor old Martha! She thinks I am the woman of Babylon now; but she is going to adore me before the summer is over. And you shall tell me about this place, so that I can find my way—I mean among the people. As for these mountains, did you ever know anything like them? I never did. They look as if they were made of sunshine and purple chiffon. I suppose they can be ugly enough when it rains, though."

" No, never, never ! "

" Oh, you love them, I see, just as I love Boylston Street, and the milliners' windows, and Englander's and the Common, and the Back Bay fens, and all. Well, you are the minister's daughter," leaning forward, her elbows on her knees, and surveying her. " I suppose you are awfully good. Who was that youth I saw then—tall, blonde, with black eyebrows, going up the road? There he is, looking round now," said Luisa, half turning to peer through the crack of the open, back-garden gate.

" That is John Donner," said Mary Swann, and the apple-blossom color became that of a damask rose.

" That is John Donner, is it ? " said

Luisa, looking at her with a bubbling laugh. "And now, tell me all about John Donner." And the two girls were on the way to be friends without more ado.

It was at the same moment that Luisa had run for the trowel that a similar sensation of pity for cribbed and cabined lives passed here touched Miss Barbara with the shiver that people say you have when some one is stepping on your grave.

"This is nonsense," said Miss Barbara, and then she wiped her reading-glasses and adjusted herself to her task.

It was not a very interesting task at first— Miss Barbara's. There were copies of various old wills and decrees of court; the Camperdouns had been a litigious race. There were deeds of land and woodland, which she examined carefully; and there were old account-books, which she handled more cursorily; and there were some diaries — brief, threadbare statements of the days of dull and simple lives; and then there were old letters.

They were yellow, and falling apart in folds, these letters. Here was one—a love-letter? Yet, in what stilted phrase! But out of it dropped a pressed and faded rose, and all the pride and passion hidden in the stately words were revealed in the flower. A tear sprang in Miss Barbara's eye; they were her own people. She felt how precious the pompous and sounding old letter once had been. Here was the epistle her grand-father had sent from the Indies, whither he had sailed, beginning, "Esteemed Wife." And, yes, here was the reply, "My Honored Husband." Were they really alive then, these people? Did their hearts beat? A still shining little lock of a dead baby's hair, that she had sent him as if he must have something to touch of the child born and dead in his absence, fell from the next letter and answered her.

Here were her own letters to her Cousin Launce, among them the one in which she had refused to marry him. "We are cousins," she had said in it, "and that might be bad enough if we were all as other people, we Camperdouns. But with the dark possibility that hangs over every one of us, it would be inviting ruin. Perhaps we would better not see each other often, if ever. I shall not marry."

His answer had been brief and to the point: "Neither shall I."

·Plainly, he had lived up to his determination. There were no love-letters from other women. There were a few business letters, on the backs of which he had noted memoranda, a passing thought, an extract of something he had been reading, one or two letters from friends—one where the signature caught her eye first, John Donner, the same name as that at the foot of the letter lately announcing her cousin's death and her inheritance; Dr. Donner telling her she was the executor of Mr. Camperdoun's will, made many years ago.

"I don't know now whether I am eavesdropping or not," said Miss Barbara. "He's alive—but it's part of the business,

I suppose. All the same —— " and she smoothed out the old letter, as she had done the others, and read :

" Thanks to you, dear boy, the work is over, and he that was Rusticus salutes you Medicus. Nor shall I be so long as I had feared in paying what it cost. I am paying what it cost now.

" I am bringing a wife to Woodsedge. That surprises you. It did me.

" Of course, you know, remembering the ' nights we had in Egypt,' that it was no thought of mine. But while I was at work, some good friends saw the chance and smoothed the way. And I simply fell in— with their suggestion. She has—let me tell you—a little pot of money. With that I shall look up my debts, and buy old Pil- cott's place and practice in Woodsedge ; I always liked that house. I shall turn the place into a stock-farm, and start a new breed of horses—do what I must in the way of my profession, and no more. And for the rest, there shall be marauding of the hills with you, and all the pleasures of our youth so long as youth lasts.

"The only trouble is that she may wish to make a man walk too straight a line. Her own lines are very straight—a girl who never was young, and who looks at life through the narrow chink of the church door. Oh, well, it's a hard world, and very few of us get out of it alive. But when I remember your flashing Cousin Barbara, when I remember the pretty girls across the hills and far away——

"There it is, old fellow. I had to pour it out or die, and you are all I have. But keep it to yourself. It is Mrs. Donner, you know. And Mrs. Donner shall be treated with respect. But a wife is not the end of the world, my boy. A hard world? No it isn't, no it isn't! It's a good, gay world! And with many a bout before us yet, I am yours to command, "JOHN DONNER."

Miss Barbara read the letter again. Somehow it made her heart stand still with a sense of the tragedy in it.

"Was the man writing about his wife?" she said, as she folded it up and put it back into the desk with the rest of the papers. "Was he writing of a woman who had given him not only her money but herself? What incredible baseness! The lout—the scoundrel! I could not have believed a man capable of it! What a contemptible thief! Can it be—it is impossible! It can't be— But it is! The man who wrote me of Launce's death; he has always been close to the poor fellow. But I don't understand. That man who met us at the station, and drove us over here with what he called his lightning-shod team; that silent man with his rugged face, his eyes that were set in his head like wells and seemed to reflect the very blue of heaven and all its beneficence — why, that man looked as if he might be a messenger of God! Dear me—it is the greatest mystery I ever came across. But there were never

two John Donners here, and he is the one
I saw breaking in that great black brute
and looking like a centaur, nearly forty
years ago, for I reminded him of it. Yes;
and he had a sort of blind worship of
Launce, I remember. Well, the longer you
live the more you know," said Miss Barbara. "I wouldn't have thought," she
presently began again, "I wouldn't have
thought any one out of state's prison
could— He ought to be in state's prison
now; that's where he ought to be! That
poor girl, that poor woman he married
—I wonder what became of her?" And
Miss Barbara's eyes wandered dreamily to
the window of the west parlor where she
sat. "Dear me!" she cried. "Do they
have countesses up here in the woods?
Who is that, I wonder?" And she surveyed with an admiring interest the figure
moving slowly up the path, and bearing a
parcel in her hands as if it were a crown
upon a cushion; a tall and slender person,
a small, white shawl upon her shoulders,

carrying herself and her napkin-covered dish with a gentle, high-bred air. "I declare," said Miss Barbara, aloud, "I should think a Copley had stepped out of a portrait, if her dress were silk and satin instead of hodden gray. Who is it, Martha?" as presently that dame opened the door, holding a platter of golden butter-balls set in great green leaves and bunches of scarlet blossom.

"She wouldn't come in, then," said Martha, "seein's you wuz jes' come, an' tired, she ses. She's jes' fetched this over in the way of you feelin' among friends. Ye needn't set nothin' in pertickler by it, though; she's doin' ez much fer ev'ybuddy. She keeps the keys fer the poor o' this perrish, an' it's a wide an' a long one," said Martha, a little defiantly, as if Miss Barbara had challenged her. "I do' know w'at she'll do in heaven with no poor nor sick nor dyin' ter be seen ter. She's been a-tendin' the wounded feet o' the Lord ever sence she set her own in this place an' come here for its best blessing, arter the doctor himself. It's Mis' Dr. Donner, ma'am.''

''Oh, Aunt Barbara,'' cried Luisa, as she came into the west parlor, where Miss Barbara was still sitting, speechless, ''I've fallen in with the loveliest girl—a real wild rose of a girl, if she wasn't so white—an exquisite creature ! But there must be something in the air here that makes people charming, for I met the most beautiful creature at the gate. She wasn't young ; she was—she was——''

''All of my age, Luisa. Say it,'' said Miss Barbara.

''And she wasn't handsome ; she wasn't pretty. She was simply heavenly looking. Oh, one of the angels bearing the Grail might have looked just so. A middle-aged angel, you know.''

''She was bearing butter in a lordly dish,'' said Miss Barbara, in reply. But to herself she said, ''And that was Dr. Donner's wife. The woman with a pot of money. Well, there's an old song I've heard that says, 'They went up through much tribulation.' Perhaps she knows what it means.''

II

It had been a very unhappy woman that came so long ago to Woodsedge, a month's bride, the wife of John Donner.

Always a silent woman, now she was stricken dumb. In the month she had discovered what her pot of money meant. If she were not absolutely sure in the matter, her suspicion was as sad as certainty.

She had lived the quiet life of her native seaport—more than ordinarily quiet, perhaps, owing to the long illness of her mother, whose death had been followed by that of her father—with few other pleasures than that of church-going, an eventless walk with a friend, an afternoon sail, maybe a lecture. Her temperament had been attuned to the calm and even tenor of the sick-room—if the sky were blue and the sun shone the pitch was rather higher than if the rain poured in a gray torrent; but when the rain poured, a little more effort was given to maintain the tone.

When she first saw John Donner, who had come down with a fellow-student from the medical school for a Sunday, something stirred in her heart which she had never felt before. She did not fairly know what it was; but perhaps under its stress her gaze rested on the young man a little longer than she was aware. When he lifted his own eyes and their glance happened to catch hers, a color dyed her face that made him look again, and the gray eyes under their straight black brows fell as swiftly. His friend saw the glance and the color, made a jest, and mentioned her money — a small enough sum of money, but riches to the young student helped to his profession by the kindness of Launce Camperdoun and others—and the rest was easy. He found that much warmth of expression was not needed; Nancy had been bred in the ways where still waters run deep, and her life took the fresh force and swung over into its new channel, and flowed along there with the strength and depth of a great river.

It was all the sweetest surprise to her. Her plain, immobile face and tall, gaunt figure, her silence, her shyness, her ignorance of the social arts, had hindered admiration and attention; she had never supposed she would have a lover. And suddenly heaven had opened to her. Certainly, in those bright days she did not feel as if she walked the earth. Yet no one would have dreamed from her serious demeanor that she was occupied with anything but a business agreement. She loved the taking, handsome scamp with her whole heart. She was glad that she had money to give him; she gave it all, and at once. She wished that she had beauty for him; but what did it signify when he was so high-minded that he did not heed its absence, and looked for an inner beauty in her soul? He imagined it there, she said in her humility; but for his sake she would make it grow there—the desert

should blossom as the rose. She made few
confidences to those about her—she hardly
made a confidant of heaven; but into her
formal prayer would sometimes escape his
name as she implored the Lord's best blessing for him, with every fibre of her being
trembling. She little dreamed the fiery
path they must tread together to reach that
blessing.

And then they were married and went
away. He had a fancy to know a little of
the wider world before going back among
the hills. He had never had the means to
do so before. He wanted to see some races,
some great stables, to buy some Kentucky
horses. She was a sort of necessary adjunct
to the journey. He was not unkind to her;
he was even kind, after a fashion—now and
then. As for her, she asked nothing more;
she did not know there was anything more
to ask; she was his; they were to be together all their lives. Perhaps her admiring
worship was not unpleasing, at first; it made
him think that he was not wholly a bad fel-

low, when he thought of it at all. Then he didn't care. Then he forgot it.

But everything was so novel, she had no time to consider herself; the great world was slipping by her like the scenes of a panorama. Instead of caresses, she contented herself with his masterful air of cool proprietorship. She was a part of this world, she no longer stood outside; she had entered into its broad currents; she was a wife, the wife of a man built on the scale of great men, noble, fine, past her imagining—alas, as yet, all of her imagining!

She lived a month in her fool's paradise. And she awoke one night in her room at the cheap hotel where he had left her while he pursued his pleasures, to see Dr. Donner sitting in a chair in the middle of the floor, his coat off and his hat on, and with other disarrangements of undress, his feet outstretched, his head hanging forward, and the gas blazing over him, lost in a drunken doze.

He woke with a start at her exclamation,

looked about in a bewildered way, and then his head fell forward again. "Sold out!" he was muttering to himself, in a thick undertone, with now and then an oath. "Thass so, Donner. Gone for a shil'n', gone! Go' the price, though," he mumbled again, fetching himself up from another doze, with a lurch on his chair. "Sma' price. Saddled with 'cumbrance. Good woman—good woman's ever was—my Nannie O," with a tipsy laugh; and one foot went up in a jig-step, to the danger of his equilibrium on the seat. "Lock self in an' los' key," he was babbling, presently again. "Go' a jailer—damn fool! Plain's they make 'em. Worse 'n a scarecrow," he exclaimed, angrily, at that. "Puts me in mind—stock-farm—horses—pot o' money," and he was nodding off again. "Treat her with respec'," he gurgled then, with another start. "Mis' Donner—no foolin'—no foolin' 'ith Mis' Donner—hear wha' I say? Pot o' money—blamed 'cumbrance, all the same! Married her money, didn't marry her!"

For half an instant she supposed it was some sudden attack of illness. With the next breath she knew all about it. But it was as if a thunderbolt had struck her. She lay cold and stiff, unable to move hand or foot, a breath out of the very iciness of death blowing over her as she gazed at him. And then her eyes grew hot with scalding tears, and she was trembling like a leaf—her idol, her idol! Everything was shattered with that, every hope, every joy. Her heart was lead. The world had come to an end. She gathered her senses with pain, to wish wildly that she were dead, that he —that he, her love, her husband, had died before this evil chance. And while she lay there half lifeless, now and again a long shudder sweeping her from top to toe, she heard these dreadful words.

To tell the truth, they affected her but little at the time. His love of her, or the contrary, was of small consequence now. That went down in all the other ruin.

But something must be done. She slipped

out of bed as soon as she could command her movements, and went to him, taking his hat, unbuttoning his collar, half holding her head away from his hideous breath, trying to remove his boots. He slowly opened and rolled his fiery eyes upon her.

" Lemme 'lone ! " he said. " Lemme 'lone—cat ! " And then, as if possessed of a sudden fury, he clenched his fist and lifted it to strike her, but paused with it doubled in the air. " No," he said. " Mis' Donner. Treat her with respec'. All the same, 'cumbrance." And he rose, swinging and steadying himself, stepped off with dignity on his heels, and fell forward on the side of the bed in a stupor.

With all her strength and all the knowledge she had gained in her long experience of handling the sick, she at last got off a portion of his clothes, had a cold-water compress on his head, covered him up, put the room in order, and throwing on her own wrapper, sat down for her dreadful vigil with her dead happiness.

It was in the gray of the morning when he awoke, with his brain emerging from the fervors that had obscured it, pushed away the compress from his aching head and saw her kneeling at the window, her hair dropping round her poor, bent face, her hands folded in an intensity of prayer, the curtain up, a great silver star shining over her in the whitening east. He looked at her a moment curiously.

"Damned rascal!" he said then to himself. "Don't deserve her. Looks like a Saint Something. Who ever heard of a Saint Nancy?" And he laughed and turned over into sleep again.

When he once more awoke, in the middle of the afternoon this time, she sat heating over a spirit-lamp a bowl of broth that she had ordered to the room. He watched her in silence. He was faint and dizzy—it seemed good to have some one caring for him. As she turned and met his eyes, he saw what havoc he had wrought in her.

"Made a beastly fool of myself last

night, Nancy!'' he said. ''Never happened before. And sha'n't happen again,''
with which two lies he meant to comfort
her. And he did.

She ran to his side and threw her arms
round him, and forgave him everything.
And then, before he could lift his hand to
caress her as he had intended, she remembered those words of his, those deadly bru-
tal betraying words of his, and rose quickly
and drew back out of his reach, frozen half
to marble.

''No,'' she said, ''I will believe you.
It was an accident. A man like you will
not let himself down to a lower level. You
will not throw away your future.''

He had expected reproaches and beseech-
ings and implorations for her sake. She
had put it all for his own sake. She didn't
cry out when she was hurt. Well, she was
something of a thoroughbred, after all.

He asked her, as soon as he was on his
feet, what she would like for some last en-
joyment before going home, expecting, of

course, she would take a gala night in all
the stir and light and color of the play.
But she chose instead to hear a preacher
who had a way of searching men's souls,
and he went along with her. It was a good
while since he had been in any church.
He was rather amused with himself. He
looked about at the people, expecting to be
amused by them, also. But whether it was
the personality of the preacher, or his mes-
sage, a light seemed to flash out of darkness
upon John Donner, and although it was
gone again directly, he had it to remember.
He had also to remember the look in his
wife's face as the great music of choir and
organ rolled over them—a look in the gray
eyes that startled him with the might of
something beyond his ken. "She shall
have a pew of her own," he promised himself.

And the next day they started for home.
Home! She half wondered at herself that
she let him call it so, and that she went
with him there. But in the long sleepless

night of her first misery she had chosen her
way. She could not go back to the place
she had left; nor had she the money to do
so; all her money was in his hands. To
be sure, she could go to work—she was
well and strong. "But I promised," she
said, "for better, for worse. I will not
break my vow because his was false. He
needs me, too. I must help him. And
oh, I cannot, I cannot leave him! Oh,
no—oh, no; I love him still!" She had
resolved before, that as he was unaware of
his revelation on that drunken night, she
would never let him know of it, or guess
that she understood what he had done, or
knew of his feeling of repugnance to her.
She would appear to take things for granted.
She had no expectation of ever changing
his feeling. That was a thing impossible,
she said, with her hopeless face, her stiff
manner, her lack of the pretty graces of
pretty women. In a day and night at a
grand hotel she had seen beautiful ladies in
beautiful toilets with a sort of alarm; if

she had had their gowns she could not have worn them so; she would not have had a notion how to dress her thin, sleek hair in the bewildering way of theirs. She comprehended that there was a fine art of dress of which she was ignorant. She saw, too, that her husband was so indifferent to her that he was not even ashamed of her poor, home-made finery. She felt as if she would like to put on black, the deepest crape of mourning, and wear it the rest of her life; she never did wear anything again but sombre tints and the gray and white which afterward became a sort of lovely fashion of her own. She had seen his glance following those women—she would be willing to be boiled in oil if she might become beautiful enough to be followed in that way by those eyes! Wild fancy, hopeless thought! And there was work to do. All that night in the rush and jolt of the cars through the defiles and up the grades of the hills, she prayed for John Donner's soul, and a passion leaped into her prayer like the fresh blood to a wound, giving it life that it seemed must bring its answer.

And so she took up the days at Woods-edge, in the old-fashioned white house upon the green, that John had always wanted and had now bought, with its paddocks and pastures up the hill behind it, on which he soon had a notable knot of horses—wild, lovely creatures, that gave a new life to the dark mountain on whose slope they galloped.

It was well for Mrs. Donner that she had her household duties to attend to, a housewife by nature and training, for otherwise she could not have endured, with all her other trouble, and the confronting of the strange women who called upon her, the presence of the dark and unfamiliar mountains. She wanted to push them off; they worried and saddened and oppressed her; she longed so for a sight, a sound, a smell of the sea, that sometimes her soul was sick within her.

But she knew that she must put a stop to

all that, for the little life that was coming
must not be clouded by the mother's
gloom; and she tried to think of everything
that was bright and beautiful, and to go
singing about her work all the glad, sweet
hymns she knew. She hung out bits of
string and wool for the building birds, and
felt as if she had friends with the other
mothers when they took them. But she
had hard work to keep her cheer.

She saw very little of her husband. She
began to be sure that he was not obeying
half the calls that she so laboriously answered at the door, and that when he came
home late at night it was not because he had
been with the sick or dying. She did not
exactly know where he had been, of course.
But in snatches of talk that she overheard
when Launce Camperdoun was about, and
in other ways, she was vaguely aware of the
existence of the tavern in between the hills,
of the race-course and trotting-park on the
intervale beyond Loon Mountain, of Dawlish's on the other side of the quaking

heath, and the roystering companions, the betting and card-playing there. As for the events that made the life of those places gay, she had no power of imagination to picture them, and she did not even conjecture them. But she had such a reverence for her husband's profession, as something that stood guard at the gates of life and death and waited on the will of God, that he was himself involved in it in a measure, even when she knew he was doing wrong; he had received a consecration ; he must in the end come out right, and she ignored all but the end.

In the meantime, as far as she could, she made up for his deficiencies by her own presence, and with little gifts out of the pantry-stores that had been sent from her old home when broken up, and out of her abundance of jellies ; and with delicate tisanes and broths from her kitchen, too, Mrs. Donner made herself welcome in many a sick-room long distances apart; and being there, it was she, who had closed her mother's and her father's eyes, who made it easier for these others to go out of life.

One night when John came home from a long bout, he found that a patient whom he had neglected and forgotten had been taken home by her where she herself could do the nursing, and where the doctor must needs be on hand more or less.

"You are a good woman, Nancy," he said, after a moment.

"I thought you would prefer it," she replied, as if it had been not his suggestion but his wish.

"But I am not going to have the house turned into a hospital for every acquaintance-in-law, with you for head nurse," he said.

"You shall if you like."

And with half an idea that it had been his wish, and with an interest that surprised himself, be bent all his skill to the cure; and Dr. Donner's resources were not small.

The people who had wondered at Dr.

Donner when he brought his wife to Woodsedge were beginning now to wonder at
themselves.

And then the long winter was at hand,
with the snows borne on whistling winds,
flying down the mountain passes and drift-
ing deep in gorges and ravines, making it
seem as if one were in a dead world. But
although she could not always hinder the
feeling of something near despair creeping
over her, she never yielded to any longing
to be dead herself. No, she desired to live
—whether he wanted her or not, she had to
live for John's sake. But he had observed
her so little that he was unaware of her con-
dition till lately, and she was alone with
the nurse who had happened in—the doctor
off on a carouse at Dawlish's—the night the
little boy was born.

It was a stinging piece of her mind that
Martha, the nurse, gave Dr. Donner when
he came home.

"That is right," he said, laughing, "and
well deserved. And then it would do you

harm to keep that to yourself—too much venom in it ! Do you know," he said, quite with the air of saying a pleasant thing, "if it was a hundred years ago you would be treated to the ducking-stool——"

"A hundred years ago or now, I know w'at you'd orter be treated to !" said Martha.

"Now," he went on, "we will see if you are as good a doctor as you are a scold." And he satisfied himself that all was right. "You have done me a good turn, Martha," he said, "and I sha'n't forget it," and then he went to bed.

But the sight of that white, patient face upon the pillow had sobered him more than Martha's words had done; and he had kissed his wife and told her she had a son that was worth it all.

He never seemed to feel that he had any share in the boy—a long, thin starveling of a child. He hardly ever looked at him except when his ailing required it. He never liked to see suffering; he was too pleasure-

loving for that.   But something sent a thrill
through him one night after his wife was
about, as he saw her sitting by the fire with
the child on her arm, a look of the rapture
of love shining on her countenance. He
stopped a moment and came back, and
lifted the blanket away from the little face.

"Nancy," he said, again, "you are a
good woman ! "

It was all he had to say, when a month
later the little weakling was laid away in a
span-long grave, that the snows had been
hollowed out to make, and she had swal-
lowed her tears, and taken home the child
of a neighbor to lie in her child's place till
the mother should be well of a blasting
fever.   "It is our little son who is giving
all he had to the baby," she said, looking
up with the sorrow still in her eyes.

" Nancy always had beautiful eyes," the
doctor thought.

And neither cock-main, nor dog-fight,
nor a dance at Dawlish's called Dr. Donner
off till the baby's mother was well enough

to take him back and leave Nancy's arms empty again.

There came to the door, not long afterward, a worthless-looking woman, with her child in the bundle she carried, and followed by a dog. She wanted help to get back to her own parish, where she would go upon the town.

"What are you doing with that trollop?" the doctor asked, as he saw his wife take her in.

"I thought perhaps we could help her," she replied. And she bathed the woman's sore feet and put her to bed; and she gave the dog a bone; and she washed the baby, a fine, crowing boy, and then went to the closet where her own baby's clothes had been put away. She could not help the tears nor the kisses she gave the dear, soft wool and cambric things, she who had nothing left to kiss. But she dressed the lucky little stranger out in them from top to toe.

"That was hard for you to do, Nancy," said the doctor, seeing her.

"I wanted our little boy to take his part in helping in the world," she replied.

"He is still alive to you, in a way." He was drinking coffee, and Nancy's coffee was a cordial.

"Oh, yes! Even if not here. And do you know," she said, timidly, and half under her breath, "does it—does it not strike you—do you never feel a sort of —oh not pride—to think you are the— father of an angel?"

"I?" roared John, with a clatter of laughter. "I? I never felt I was the father of a child. You and he are too good for me, I guess."

But it was, perhaps, a new wonder he felt concerning his wife, when he found that Sally with her boy and the dog Brow stayed on in Nancy's kitchen. They were staying there many a long year after.

Lonely or longing or sorry now, Nancy could not let herself be cast down. The house must be kept cheerful for its master's sake. And then there was so much ready for her hand to do. In those days, and in that remote region, nurses were not to be had for the asking, and friends and neighbors helped out the need of every family when sickness came; the squire's wife and the minister's served their turn, and already there was no one in all the township who had such a name for a good watcher as Mrs. Donner had. But often in the dead waste and middle of the night she drew aside the curtain of the sick-room to look out on the snowy wilderness and the white hillside where her baby lay. It was so hard that the cold snow should cover him, her little darling, when her heart yearned so to warm him on her breast! But she said to herself that God hides His flowers in the bosom of the earth till summer shines again; and she remembered pictures she had seen where the clouds about heaven were full of children's faces. Sometimes she saw the full moon hang over that little grave like a great presence of brooding motherliness; and she grew to love the solemn encampment of the

hills round about it, and the dark-green firs
that now and then shook down an avalanche
of crusted snow with a far sweet thunder;
and the stars seemed to come and go between the great purple crests, like spirits
keeping watch about that one little spot.
Occasionally, when some member of the
family rose early, that she might go home
and have a short rest herself before it was
yet light, she met her husband coming in
the dawn from Dawlish's, or from some of
the cabins beyond Loon Mountain. If he
were any way ashamed, he was still sufficiently master of himself to be a little entertained by the situation; and it was a
curious glance he gave her then out of the
corner of his eyes, as something he could
not make out or understand. But he knew
perfectly well that she was supplementing
his work—sometimes supplying its absence.

It happened that once or twice in a way
Dr. Donner, for some reason or other,
whether compassion or a divine curiosity,
had warmed to his work, had searched out

many inventions to serve a patient, faithful
by night and day with a faithfulness that
fatigued his unwonted spirit, leaving no
power of his will or secret of his art unused ;
but nature being too strong for him, or the
abuse of nature, the case had lapsed into
failure ; and then the people whom he had
attended were bitter about his methods and
slandered his skill, and took care that he
should know it. "And I must spend my
life and waste my youth and be made a
target for these blunderbusses!" he cried.
"Oh, you know their calibre, Launce, but
you can't know their bore!" It used to
cut him to the quick, however, as the reproaches he had deserved had never cut
him, and his wife's resentment and fellow-
feeling then were a balm to his heart.
They gave him a kindlier mood in her regard, that desired her sympathy and forbearance, and did more for her with him
than all her simple goodness did.

If people were often indignant with Dr.
Donner, they were, on the whole, patient.

There was no one else very near; they regarded his talent as prodigious, his healing power as something special to himself. Now and then, if rarely, an interest in some malady seemed to take him and absorb him; now and then he wrought some miracle. They fell into a way of saying that when the need was great enough Dr. Donner was always there.

"The merest nonsense!" he said to his wife once, when he felt some extenuation necessary, a thing that a short time since would not have occurred to him. "Brown-bread pills and a phial of clear water will work half the cures, and when I let them alone I am only helping nature do her own work."

"But there is more," she said, a little surprised at herself, yet perhaps taking courage because Launce Camperdoun was at the table. "To be a physician is to make a promise that one would give——"

"Everything required of a physician. Well, I do," he said, in high good humor.

"I give them you. I do one part, you do the other. But look here, old lady, take care you don't encroach."

"Encroach!" she exclaimed, before she thought. "I should as soon think of encroaching on the work of heaven! Oh, you know," she said, setting down her cup, "a doctor's work is the work of heaven. He holds so many hearts in his hand. He gives life or death. He gives hope, comfort, relief. The people feel safe thinking of him. They lean on him. They love him. He brings them into the world, he makes the way easy for them going out. Even pain obeys him. He forgets himself. The weather doesn't hinder him. Sick or well, storm or shine, he is all the time doing the work of his Master. Oh," she added, looking up across the table, her face aglow, "I didn't mean to say so much, but it seems to me that there is no one in the world stands so near the Lord as he does——"

"Hold on, hold on!" cried John, with

a slightly difficult laugh. "Is it possible that I am all this?"

"You must be. You are under doctors' vows."

"By George, Nancy! You are enough to put the spirit of it into a man!"

"You builded better than you knew when you married that woman," said Launce, as they went out together.

"By God, I did!" said John.

He did not think it was encroaching when, a few weeks later, having left a patient in extremity and forgotten how the time passed, he came back to find the mother resting comfortably with the newborn baby beside her, and his wife in attendance, she having gone when the third summons for him came, feeling she must risk everything both for the woman and in his behalf.

There was not room for two in the gig, and he walked home in the thick night beside her, the horse's head over his shoulder.

"How did you know how?" he asked, presently.

"I didn't," she said. "But I had been with three or four cases, you know. And I had my own experience. I was expecting Martha every minute, and she came at the very last. And Mrs. Janes had to be taken care of. And oh, John, you had to be protected, too! And I just prayed God to help me. And it was life, and not death, you know, and that helped, too."

"That is the way God helped," said John, in a low voice. "Well, Nancy, you have saved me this time!"

She went for the lantern, that he might put up the horse. He took it, and stooped and lifted her hand to his lips. She laughed, with a kind of childish pleasure. He swung the ray of the lantern up across her face.

"You are growing prettier every day, Nan," he said.

"No," she answered, suddenly pale and cold again, "I am growing an old woman.

But we are very good friends, I think, John.''

It happened that the next day was Sunday. Nancy always went to meeting, and would have done so even had it not been expected that everyone in that community should regard the day as one of solemn ceremony, except the doctor, who in a measure was excused by reason of his duties. Save for the Sunday, now so long ago, when he brought her home, Dr. Donner had taken advantage of his privileges.

''See Mis' Donner,'' said Deacon Ashly to his wife, as they jogged home together, '' w'en the doctor come inter meetin' ter-day? She looked 'sif 'twouldn't take much to make her drop. Kinder took by s'prise, mebbe.''

''Sho! I guess nothin' he could du 'd take her by s'prise. She's jest all tuckered out, being 'th Mis' Janes overnight. Miry Dean was tellin' me between meetin's. He's be'n tendin' out on her, an' I s'pose she thought Mis' Janes was gone.''

"He tol' me himself Mis' Janes wuz right as a trivet. So 'twarn't thet. But I'll tell ye what I think, Mis' Ashly; I think Dawlish's'll hev seen the last o' Dr. Donner afore long!"

"I'll believe it w'en I see it," said Mrs. Ashly, grimly.

"A good wife goes a great way to the makin' of a good man, Mis' Ashly," said the deacon.

"Good or bad, Deacon Ashly," said the worthy dame, with decision, "there's never be'n a doctor here between the hills that was Donner's beat. Old Dr. Pilcott was well enough w'en he knowed jes' w'at ailed ye, but Donner looks right inter the marrer. I do' know's I'd like to trust myself in his han's w'en that black horse o' his'n takes him home 'cause he can't drive himself. But if I did, he'd fetch me thru!"

"P'r'aps so, p'r'aps so," said the deacon. "But fer my part, I like the man thet hes ter tend my mortle body or my immortle sperrit ter hev all his wits about him."

"Wal, part o' Dr. Donner's wits is more'n most men-folks hes. Ef he allus hed the hull on 'em about him we shouldn't keep him long up here 'tween the hills. They'd be a-wantin' of him down ter Boston quicker'n scat. I do' know es it's very profitable talk we're a-havin', Deacon Ashly. Did you see Miry's new shawl? I noted the fringe warn't es long es mine by an inch. Hm. That's a cur'us text the preacher hed this mornin'. I allus thought it was a pretty varse. 'Woe unto the drunkards of Ephraim, whose glorious beauty is a fading flower.' 'Twas a good sarmon, though."

"S'archin'," said the deacon, "s'archin'!"

Whether Dr. Donner found it searching or not, the next Sabbath his wife, who had hitherto been the guest of the often empty Camperdoun pew, sat in a pew of her own, carpeted and cushioned in a way to alleviate that mortification of the flesh for which the village congregation had apparently arranged the straight backs and narrow seats, and on which they would have looked with disfavor had it been for any one but Mrs. Donner.

III

IT was at about this time that the epidemic of fatal influenza broke out in Woodsedge. There was no loitering possible then, no time, if it were wished, for any life at Dawlish's, for any running of horses, for any meeting of sports between the hills; the calls were too frequent, too urgent, the need was too apparent. But Dr. Donner rose to the moment. He had forty cases on his hands at once. If he lost very few, it was due as much to his wife as to himself, he said to someone afterward. "I hate to tell you," she would say, when he came home from a round of calls on patients desperately ill, at midnight, wet through, perhaps, and tired to the ends of his fingers, " but there are three other calls for you, and they all seem to need you so. There are your dry clothes hanging by the fire for you to change. And you must take this thick, hot soup first. Mrs. Ashly is doing nicely. And I left the minister an hour ago sleeping like a baby." And while he was gone she kept the fire alive, getting her naps only on the sofa, and was bright and ready for him, sometimes with a hot breakfast, when he came back.

"It is dreadful," she sighed. "I am afraid you will be down yourself. But it seems as if you must go. I feel—oh, I hope it isn't wicked !—I almost feel as if you had only to say *Talitha cumi*, and they rise and walk."

"Not I ! Not I !" said John. "So far from it that when I come to the bedsides of the people, with nothing but my small skill between them and the power of the pest, I feel like a worm with a foot hanging over me. And when I have made a cure, if I have made it, I only feel like the same worm that the foot has failed to tread on ! "

Fortunately, the epidemic had passed, and

the mild spring weather had brought hope
and cheer, before Launce Camperdoun fell
ill.

Whether the letter from his Cousin Barbara had had anything to do with his con-
dition or not, the fever that presently appeared increased, with symptoms involving
the brain that gave the doctor a great deal
of alarm. He had the more alarm that he
knew the idiosyncrasy of the Camperdouns,
and the danger there when the brain was
called in question. For Launce Camperdoun had been his friend from long ago, his
intimate even when he was employed on the
big farm breaking the Camperdoun colts,
his companion afterward in all those times
when they had heard the chimes at midnight, the strength, the daring, the fresh
earthiness of the one feeling the subtlety and
delicacy of a failing race in the other with
almost a passionate sensibility. When
Launce came into the property, knowing
John Donner's parts, he had helped him to
his profession, often going down for a wild

beat together about the town, where John always lost his way. "It takes heredity to know the Boston streets," John used to say. And he had seen with Launce now and then at the Camperdoun cousin's house what lovely women and gracious manners are. Now the doctor called up all he knew, cursed the time that he had been playing instead of learning more, bent to use every energy he had, sent for older doctors in consultation, let other patients get along as they could, lost no moment and no endeavor in the struggle with this devouring fire, and hardly left the house by day or night unless upon compulsion of some more exacting or pitiable demand, worn and weary himself to exhaustion, every throb of that tortured brain striking like a sharp blow upon his own sensation.

Martha, the nurse, came to help him, and stayed afterward the remainder of the man's life. But he had sent her to rest that day, and it seemed to the doctor as if a minister of light had come into the room when his wife closed the door behind her and said, softly, " They have sent for you to go down to Three Rivers—the Judge's child. The ride in the wind will help you. I can keep on the ice-cap and the warm applications, and give the drops and attend to the nourishment. I am not afraid of his delirium. I am strong. You can trust me." And he went, with a sort of preknowledge that on returning he should find Camperdoun better for that calm and cooling presence. And he did. There was something about Nancy that carried healing in its wake.

I don't know why it occurred to Dr. Donner to do as he did just then, except for a freak of light-heartedness at his patient's improvement. "He does not look as I expected," he said, beckoning her into the next room. " Has he had the drops from the blue phial? If you have forgotten I told you to give them I wouldn't give that for his life ! " as he snapped his fingers.

"Oh! It isn't possible ! " whispered Nancy, clasping her hands.

"What isn't possible? Do you mean to tell me you forgot them?" flashing on her a strange glance from those keen blue eyes.

"Yes," she said, pale even in the half-light of the curtained place.

"Think a moment. You may not remember now. Perhaps you did give them at half-past three," closing the door as he spoke.

"No," she said, with white lips. "I did not. Oh, do something! Oh, save him, John!"

"Save him?" he repeated, laughing, taking her hand and leading her to a seat. "You have saved him! He doesn't look as I expected—he looks a great deal better. And, of course, you haven't forgotten because I never told you to remember!"

"Oh!" she said, pressing her fingers on her eyes to keep the tears from spurting. "It has startled me so."

"You mean I have. It was cruel," said John, still looking at her steadily. "But I wanted to try you. To see if you would tell a lie——"

" No, no ! oh, no ! "

" You will not, I see, to help yourself. I wonder if you would to help me."

"Oh, don't you, don't you ask me ! "

" But if I were in difficulty about — Well, I will put it to you. If I am called into court for malpractice—that broken arm of Miss Turpey's — and your testimony would clear me, testimony about which I would instruct you——"

" And not true ? "

" Not true, of course."

" Oh, don't let me be summoned ! " she cried, her hand over her mouth the next moment. " Oh, John, don't let me be tried so ! I could not ; oh, I could not ! "

" You would rather I went to prison, then ! "

" Oh, no, no, no ! I would not testify against you. I would be silent——"

" That would be contempt of court ; and you would go to prison yourself."

" I could go. I could be as happy there as anywhere. But, oh, if you could spare me that ! " she half sobbed. " I have tried to be a good wife—a helpmeet—to do my duty——"

" A good wife ! You are my good angel ! People call you Dr. Donner's good angel ! " And he leaned forward and kissed off the two great tears rolling down her face. " By George ! but tears are salt," he said, laughing. " There, there, I'm a hardened villain, very like, but there's no such case. I only wanted to see what is this stuff you are made of. I never saw anyone just like you, Nancy. I believe you are descended from one of the children Christ laid his hands on ! " and although she knew it was profane she felt that it was pleasant.

If she were a little angry, she was also a little glad. ˙ She never forgot, though, that he had no love for her—the sense of those old, wicked words of his was seldom out of her consciousness. But she was glad that he felt not unkindly toward her. She alternated the watches with him after that, till the immediate danger was over. And when the doctor was going on his daily rounds again, she came across the green with her little tempting dish, or her kindly pleasant talk, and let Martha off for an hour; an hour in which she made the weak and sad man feel as if he had a home, and envy the other man who had married the girl of straight lines for her money.

It was Mrs. Donner who detected first in Camperdoun's melancholia symptoms of the degeneration that the doctor had dreaded. "There is only one thing to do," said John, "and that is to reduce him to an animal, feed, and overfeed, cushion these rasped nerves in fat, and send new red blood to enrich the exhausted brain."

"Yes," said Nancy. "And he will always be subject to attack?"

"You will have it to see to as long as he lives," said the doctor, looking at her carefully.

"It is very little to do," she said. "I am glad to do it."

"My poor wife!" he said, "you married into trouble. But if there is any way known under heaven among men to hinder his becoming a victim to the family curse— But there isn't; no, there isn't! And, Nancy—somehow it hurts me—if I had been a better man he might have gone up with me instead of down—God knows! But what's done is done, and what's to do is still to do. Possibly Camperdoun would have been much the same, anyway."

"I understand," said Mrs. Donner.

"But I could give myself in his place," the doctor went on, more as if to himself than to her, "and that's a fact! I never had anyone very near me since I was in boots. I think I have loved Camperdoun more than any living thing. You care for him, too, Nancy. By mighty! he thinks well of you!"

It was like a cold hand on her heart when he said he loved Camperdoun so dearly. But why be foolish? She knew that already. And it was something that he made her so kindly his confidante—and then he had called her his wife!

The doctor came in one twilight when she had been with Camperdoun, as usual, an hour or two. He had been inclined to violence, and she had soothed him, singing. She sat beside the brooding man, and sang,

> " Art thou weary, art thou languid,
>   Art thou sore distressed?
> Come to me, saith One, and coming,
>   Be at rest."

It was not much of a voice, hardly more than a sweet and gentle sigh set to tune.

> " If I ask him to receive me,
>   Will he say me nay?
> Not till earth, and not till heaven
>   Pass away!"

But as Dr. Donner paused and flung himself into an arm-chair in the shadow, and saw her singing, the light on her face, white and wan, with a something pathetic about the mouth, but with lifted eyes that

seemed looking into heaven, he understood
that she was doing her work neither for love
of him now nor for love of the sufferer, but
for the love of God, and only the love of
them in him. "And I might have had the
heart of that woman," he thought; for he
knew his deserts too well to suppose she
could be caring for him now after the life
he had led her these three years. And then,
in a greater humility, the soul within him
cried, "But what am I, that such a spirit
bearing such a light walks through my life
at all?" and he stole out as softly as he had
entered. Opening his door that night, he
was for the first time struck by the difference between the interior of his house and
that of the old Camperdoun mansion. He
had bought the place of the Pilcott heirs, as
it stood, bare but comfortable, and what
pleasant look it had was owing only to
Nancy's home-making qualities. "It isn't
fit for her!" he exclaimed to himself. And
when she came home from some of her calls
of mercy one night, a print of Guercino's

Aurora hung over the fire in the parlor, and Murillo's Madonna, with the moon beneath her feet, was looking down from the mantel of the sleeping-room. And after that, bit by bit, a vase, a cast, a lovely book, appeared in the house. "He likes pleasant things about him," thought Nancy. He had married her so viciously, he had neglected her so long, he could not tell her they were for her.

One evening, when Camperdoun was quite himself again, Dr. Donner found his wife reading, as often before, to the convalescent, and talking in the intervals in the confidential way that had grown up between them. He waited a moment in the adjoining room. She was not a woman, as you know, of much culture or of more than average mental quality, but she had far more than the average capacity for loving.

It was a little volume of Wordsworth she was holding; she had been reading some of the ballads that she felt had a kinship with the life of this hill country. "We

used to parse this in school," she said,
"'The Happy Warrior.' I wonder if you
will understand how it makes me think of
my husband."

"Of John!" cried Camperdoun.

"I don't mean altogether what he is—
though he is so much," she said, a little
timidly, "but of what he might be—will
be. I think of him," she said, opening
the book again and reading, "as one

"'Who, doomed to go in company with Pain,
    And Fear, and Bloodshed, miserable train!
    Turns his necessity to glorious gain,'

"And then
            "'More able to endure
    As more exposed to suffering and distress;
    Thence, also, more alive to tenderness.'

"And you yourself must see," she said,
turning the leaf, "that his

"'—powers shed round him in the common strife,
    Or mild concerns of ordinary life,
    A constant influence, a peculiar grace.'

"And he never goes out in the night but I
say to myself,

" ' Or if an unexpected call succeed,
   Come when it will, is equal to the need.'

"Yes, yes," she said, still running her
eye along the page, "it is true of him all
through ! And I know, I know, that when
the end comes he will be the man who,

" ' While the mortal mist is gathering, draws
   His breath in confidence of Heaven's applause.' "

"But, man alive," said Mr. Camperdoun,
"that is about a soldier."

"And John is a soldier. You know—
if he—if he has anything to encounter in
himself and his surroundings," said Nancy,
hesitatingly. "And there are the forces of
nature he has to fight as he goes about the
hills in sun and storm and wind and rain,
by night and day. And there are the
forces of evil in pain and suffering and sorrow that he fights with," she exclaimed.
"And sometimes he fails, and so much
more often they go down ! "

"Well, well, then, you are an eloquent
little cuss—I mean customer. I beg your

pardon, Mrs. Donner.   John Donner is a
lucky dog ! ''

But as John Donner stood up and groped
his way out, he was not so sure of that.
And it was something very like a hoarse
sob one might have heard if walking home
behind him.   How could he, who had married and abused this woman so, tell her
now the truth ? He trembled before the
thought of it.

He went out on another call presently,
however. The profession he had chosen
was compelling him to recognize its power.
He found himself feeling as deep an interest
in his cases as if he saw the action of a
drama with mighty agents on the board.
It began to make him melt among his kind,
as if he were to be poured out and spent in
their service.   He had never been quite the
same since the night Janes broke down,
when he told him his wife would win
through, and had cried, and, greatly to his
embarrassment, kissed both his hands, sur-
prising him as much as if a side of sole

leather had suddenly showed human feeling. It was directly afterward that he had been called to the little girl scalded past help, the only child left to her mother, a gay-hearted Irish woman, shut into a dark hut in the notch of the hills. "Mother of God!" the woman was wailing, "you saw your own child suffer, so you did. But he was a man grown, more betoken! Whist now, Biddy, darlint, it's tearing the harrt out of me, ye are!"

The child's eyes, pools of darkness and pain, turned on him with a look that filled his own with tears; and the sight of her torment, the clenching of her little hand on his, broke up all the fountains of his pity.

"Bridget, I would bear it for her if I could!" he said, with a sudden persuasion that he would, and had gently put the little child into her last sleep; and the love that could die for another on the cross itself had for the first time a personal reality in his thought. The reality of it grew stronger when he saw Mrs. Morris, in the throes of an agony that was taking her into her grave, murmuring hymns and verses that had given her comfort, leaning on the divine assurance as if upon a bed of roses, and herself inspiring his terrible knife with courage. At the beginning he had been used to say that in the presence of any such anguish there could be no omnipotent power that was not also a malignant one ; but now he had a vision of the strength given and the heights scaled by suffering.

But while he was gone to his patient, on the night when he had heard his wife reading from the " Happy Warrior " to Camperdoun, Nancy came home and saw her crab-cactus in its full flush of pendulous bloom, and although the early November dark had fallen, she threw on her shawl again to take the pot, as it had often gone before, a little missionary flower, to the house of a sick person who had so much that all she could give her was the blossoming of this plant.

When she came out of the house again,

having done her errand, a bright light
streaming through the mist from a knoll apparently not far away attracted her; and
thinking of forest fires and their dangers,
she walked on a little way in their direction
outside the village, without remembering
that it was the night the boys up there built
their Guy Fawkes bonfires, according to the
custom still surviving in a few towns, their
fathers taking advantage of the frolic to get
their brush and rubbish burned.

She was not unhappy as she went; the
constant undercurrent of her feeling was that
she had boundless goodness to be grateful
for in the growing change in her husband's
life and in his different manner toward her.
She never suffered herself to be misled by
that; he was naturally a kind man; but she
had heard the truth from his own lips. All
the more she yearned in her affection and in
spite of herself longed for his love. When-
ever she had looked at any pretty girl upon
the way, she had felt as if there were no
physical pain, no other possible disaster, she

would not be glad to undergo, if she might come out as fair as that and have her husband regard her as the minister regarded the rosy, beaming thing he had brought home.

She was not thinking of any of this, however, but that she ought to turn back now ; when suddenly a score of bonfires sprang out of the darkness on the ledges of the neighboring hills, shadowy figures running before them with a gypsy-like suggestion. She paused, turning from one to another, and then, starting to retrace her steps, found herself bewildered as to the way, for there was neither moon nor star, and the November mists gave a sort of weirdness to the fires. She went on presently in what she supposed the right direction, hesitating at last with a strange sense of unacquaintance even in the gloom. She was not one, however, that often allowed herself to fear, and she went on again, sure that she must presently come upon some way-mark, and suddenly stopped with one foot in water and the other on yielding moss, and found that in some incomprehensible way she had taken the wrong turn, and had reached the first edge of the great quaking heath, on the border of the town, the terror of the mothers in the place, but where the more daring went for blueberries in the summer-time, the heath which was only a bed of moss and peat lying on a subterranean lake. She stood still then, for it would not do to move and plunge into she knew not what, and after a minute or two she began to call for help, nothing answering her but the echoes of her voice beating from hill to hill with airy music that had no sound of music to her.

Still, there was not any danger, unless a wildcat, or something of the sort, came down from the mountains. She stooped and groped with her hands for a hummock, found one directly beside her that seemed dry and firm, and sat down and waited, every now and again calling, and experiencing a kind of awe of the flapping echoes. She was not afraid; she was usually not at all afraid of

death in the abstract. If it had not been
for feeling that John must not be left, she
would never, in these years of her marriage,
have closed her eyes at night without a wish
that she might not unclose them in the morning. But the loneliness and darkness now
filled her with vague horror, and she left off
calling and began singing softly to herself
the hymns she loved best, as if she surrounded herself with their sacred power,
and with perhaps some of the same feeling
as that which once used certain rites and ob-
servances to keep evil spirits at bay.

But when Dr. Donner returned, as the
nine-o'clock bell was ringing, and found his
wife neither awaiting him, as usual, nor
coming in presently, he made inquiry of
Sally, and was concerned to find that she
was already concerned, as there was no very
sick person for Mrs. Donner to forget herself
over, and, moreover, she had said she would
be back directly. He went once or twice to
the window, shielding it from the bright
firelight that, painting upon the outer dark-

ness the scene within, gave him a fleeting thought of life itself as something unreally painted on the darkness. Tea had been waiting a long while. He went to the door, and looked up and down into the night. He remembered how not long since he would have laughed at the thought of this anxiety, and he hated the man that he had been.

But after a while he had found it impossible to wait, and he sallied forth again to find her and come home with her; and by eleven o'clock he had called at every door in the east end of the village, growing more and more alarmed with his own alarm, and shortly finding himself surrounded by the lanterns of fifty people following the highway, separating down this and that lane, coming together again, men and women alike, calling her name, listening for a halloo, full of excitement and fear, he himself silent, and as if he had in him the repressed force of a whirlwind.

Suddenly Sally darted past him, following Brow, the dog, with his nose down. And the doctor then was after them breathlessly, all the lanterns dancing and sparkling behind him, and in their light, before she caught sight of him, he saw Nancy sitting on the hummock in the marsh, white and calm, as she sang her hymn and stopped quickly at Brow's baying and leaping and caressing. In an instant he had sprung across and reached her and clasped her in his arms. "Oh, my wife, my darling!" he was exclaiming. And she looked up in amazement, for his tears were streaming over her cheek.

Mrs. Donner had never expected to be so happy, in all her life before, she never expected then to be so happy again as she was that night when, friends and neighbors gone after their glad entertainment, her husband, kneeling on the rug before her, as she sat by the fire, drew her face down and kissed her on the mouth—the long, deep, silent kiss of perfect love.

"I thought I had lost you, Nancy," he half sobbed in pity of himself. "I never knew life could be such a desert. Oh, you must teach me to be good as you are, half as good as you are, and to deserve the mercy I have had, my wife, my wife!"

But in his arms out there on the edge of the morass, half a flashing thought with her had been followed by remembrance that he was never to dream she knew he had married her as he did. And here in this ecstatic moment, while her transfigured face glowed in the firelight almost like a thing of beauty, unaware of change and development in himself the consciousness possessed him that this precious being was never to be so hurt as to be allowed to dream that her marriage had been desecration, that he loved her more now than he had always loved her, other than in the knowledge that love grows and increases as the flower grows from the bud, as the flame swells from the well-fanned fire, as the world grows from shapeless nebula to star.

But it was only to John Donner's eyes that beauty blossomed in this pale face. To the rest of the small village world there was no change in Mrs. Donner; they wanted none, indeed. Pure goodness and the light of a great happiness made that face fair enough for them.

Life then began again for John Donner. He knew that he had been delivered from evil. He felt that it was for a purpose. All along of late he was aware that he had been taking this in hand and taking that to please Nancy. Suddenly, whether he had caught the habit from life with her, from growing sympathy, or whether a miracle had been wrought, his endeavor was to please a higher power. It was Nancy who had said a doctor did God's work in the world, and here he was doing it with an eager, silent joy; doing it all the more that his life with Nancy seemed a part of it. Sickness and suffering and sorrow loomed before him so appallingly that he felt as if threescore and ten years would be too few for his share of the work. Although he still bred and sold his horses, the race-course beyond Loon Mountain knew him no more. The Break o' Day house forgot him. He went over to Dawlish's when they sent for him, and helped a man there wallowing in abject fear back to life again. He was friendly as before; he had no right to be otherwise, he said; he had been one of them—only the Lord had given him Nancy. But they all knew the difference there; they excused him. "A man ain't any business foolin' 'ith dead an' dyin', and 'ith us, too," they said.

"It's the same Johnny," said one of the girls, "only he's gittin' his fun out'n the other thing."

"I guess a man ain't seen fer long the misery a doctor has, to be as light as Johnny Donner uster be," said an older woman. "That night he took the mortal pain off'n my baby I says to myself, says I, 'That man won't be settin' 'em up long at Dawlish's,' says I."

"Tut, tut, tut, then," remarked the old white-headed crone sucking her pipe in the corner. "Ain't you got eyes? Johnny Donner has gone on."

"He's hed his part 'ith publishers an' sinners, I guess," said the woman with the baby. "Granny's right; he's gone on."

He was driving home one night from behind Loon Mountain, where he had done some surgical work, while the people there were in their turn discussing him.

"Don't see much o' Johnny Donner now," one said. "They say he's got religion. But he's got the same twinkle into his eye, fer all I see."

"P'r'aps it's religion," argued another, whittling his tobacco; "but w'en I see him do that lightning act 'ith his knives an' bandages, it looked the leastestest mite 'sif he'd sold his soul to the Old Boy, it did!"

"Wal," drawled the patient from his cot, "I do'no' w'ether he's got religion or religion's got him; but ef you'd ben whar I were this time yesterday, you'd 'a' thought 'twas the han's o' the livin' Lord a-draggin' of you out o' hell; you'd 'a' wanted them to hold on their grip. You'd 'a' knowed that man's made fer suthin' else than the nights at the Break o' Day.''

Perhaps in less coarse phrase this was presently the sentiment of all Woodsedge and its dependencies.

One year followed another, and you would have said that Dr. Donner had forgotten there was anything in the world but sickness and suffering, except for the joy within his own doors—for all around his wife in her deep happiness now there was the calm of perfect peace. And when little John was born, he seemed himself to enter a sacrament with God and his wife and his son. He had not greatly loved at the time the little motherling who lay on the hillside; he loved him now with a reflex love—he was Nancy's child; he was the brother of little John. He had the figure of a small, sculptured angel set up there in shining stone, and took Nancy to see it, with the new baby in her arms, turning the corner of dark cedars to come suddenly upon it.

You knew the pulse of Woodsedge presently as you met the doctor. There was fine weather and but slight ailing when you saw him in the chaise with Nancy and the baby. There was little or nothing the matter with people when you saw him, a year or two later, with the boy in the chaise, and Brow sitting upright on guard beside him. Things were not so very serious with the health of the hills when you saw him plodding along, with Brow following. But when you saw him alone in his gig, his head bent down, his face brooding, driving the successor of Satan as if his namesake were after him, you knew there was work to do, and that Dr. Donner was doing it.

Time and work, watching and waiting and weather made his features rugged, and powdered hair and beard, but his forehead kept its whiteness, his eyes their keen glow. There was no house or hearth for twenty and more miles around where the dwellers had not grown to regard him as they would a direct vicegerent of heavenly power.

Here, as the long day broke with its stretch of pain, he was sure to come and fill the morning with hope. Here, as the dark drew on with its awful shadow and dread, he brought help to bear it, courage for these, and blessed sleep and surcease of pain for those. Here, when the need was bitter, he had given not only such science and effort as he had, but he gave himself, staying night and day and night again, lost in the fight with pain and grief, with despair and death, with dark and terrible destinies. The people felt as if there were life-giving, health-compelling power in his touch, that those eyes of his could penetrate to the root of hidden evil; they had been born into his hands, their dead had died in his arms. Some of the older ones said there had been wild stories of Dr. Donner in his youth; but they seemed to have forgotten what they were. The younger ones had the more confidence in him it may be because of that; they remembered no time when he had not been there, possessing all their trust; they felt as they would had he been a figure up-holding the sky—that the sky would fall without him. One and all, when he went by, said, "There goes a good man," the feeling so fervent that it burned away all but the simplest phrase.

He had prospered, too, as the world goes. For, although Dr. Donner had collected but little money, what was left of Nancy's had increased in his care; a stretch of forest on the north of the hills, that he had always owned, had brought him revenues which, with a mica mine he opened in connection with others, had made him rich. With the years his boy had grown to manhood, perhaps not brilliant, but on the whole satisfactory, stalwart and sturdy, a handsome youth, who came home from Dartmouth to have a run through Europe. Death had not knocked at his door, and he had been able to keep Camperdoun in a fair measure of content and cheer till the end came. The very vagaries of his youth had deepened his knowledge and influence and sympathy. Now past his fiftieth year, if the serious side of life had subdued some of the old gayety of nature, a tenderness had grown into the seldom smile; and the bent head, the broad shoulders, made one who gazed at him think of Titanic strength and intensity of power.

And while all this was accomplishing, and the people had grown in their devotion to him, he had grown through his devotion to his wife. He remembered well the day when driving alone in the deep gloom of overhanging woods he had climbed the narrow green way and come out upon a burst of light, and as if he had received some spiritual revelation,_ thinking of Nancy he had passed to the worship of that which Nancy worshipped. It was something that never left him. As he went his way in the starry nights, the hollows of the midnight blue were full of a divine presence; going between the high hill pastures where the skies stretched long wastes of lonely light, it was with him; and he felt its companionship in the solitary drives from hill to hill in moonless nights, wrestling with wild snow-storms and whistling winds. And yet perhaps he never had any sweeter and loftier moment than when in the meeting-house, with the blue sky shining through the bare windows on the white walls, and glittering on white cloth and silver tankard, in his place as deacon, a place his other duties seldom allowed him to fill, he passed the bread and wine to his wife, and entered with her into the presence of God.

And this was the man, this was the woman, round about whose happiness Miss Barbara Camperdoun encamped with all her forces.

IV

"IF I had had any idea it was like this I wouldn't have made Aunt Barbara's life such a burden to her before we came up here," said Luisa, when she had found her breath again after the climbing, still feeling as though her lungs were made of red-hot brass, and had thrown herself upon the flat rock of the summit.

"Why, what did you think it was like?" said the young man standing beside her and looking over the distance.

"Oh—cows—and stubbly pastures—and people who say 'heouw.'"

"You were not very wrong. There are cows and pastures here. And there are people who say 'heouw.' So there are in Virginia, and in Iowa, and in Texas. It seems to be one consentaneous point of national dialect. But you see there is something more. My father says that if the view of the promised land was as fine as this, the prophet ought to have been satisfied with that.''

She glanced up at the young man as he stood there at his ease, leaning slightly on his long staff, but no more fatigued than if he had strolled down a lane, and gazing off at the sea of hills below them, a vast welter of green and purple melting into the horizon's azure, with every here and there out of cloud or shower sudden rainbows springing, flaming, disappearing. There was something in young John Donner's face that held Luisa's glance, notwithstanding the marvel beneath them, as if it were the light of a sun she had never seen, a gladness of gazing where the very soul shone through in beauty.

"What is it you see?" she cried. "I never see anything like that!"

"Why not?" said he, turning a little and smiling down at her. "You have eyes."

"But I see not," said Luisa. "What were you thinking of then?"

"I? Oh, but that doesn't matter."

"What were you thinking of?"

"Must I say? I was thinking of a temptation in a high mountain, and wondering if heaven were so beautiful that the kingdoms of the earth paled before them; such a kingdom as this scene, for instance."

"And what else?" as he paused.

"Well, I was gathering a hint of the Lord's city out of the golden mists over there in the east, and thinking that after all they belonged to earth, and I, too, and that if earth was to be transfigured into heavenly likeness I must do my share——"

"Do you know, if you were in Boston I should call you a prig! You are very religious, are you not?" said Luisa, still looking up at him gravely.

"As you are," he said.

"I religious?" cried Luisa. "Well! I'm the dancingest girl in Boston!"

He laughed. "Perhaps you might be that, and religious, too," he said.

"No, indeed!" she replied, turning away and gathering the broken pebbles about her. "To be religious for me means to go down to North Street and the South Cove, you know, and over the other side of the hill generally. No time for dancing, or for anything but picking up sick old women and dirty babies."

"That is one way, truly. But there are a great many paths to heaven, and travellers on the way—those who see the city and hearten others as they go; those who dream dreams and have visions——Well, perhaps you are right," abandoning himself to the confidential moment. "You can't be conscious of the great joy and not want to help others up to its experience."

"Oh, I hate the whole thing!" she cried. "It means death and dying and after death. I don't want to think of it; I don't want to hear about it!"

He looked at her and laughed again.

"You are a brand to be snatched from the burning," he said. "You can't live long in the same town with my mother and feel that way."

"But I like here."

"So do I."

"And this life, this earth, are good enough for me."

"She will show you how to live on earth, and in heaven, too."

"Do you?" she exclaimed.

"I am not as good as my mother. Hardly anyone could be," he said, gently.

"Your mother! Oh, what a horrible time your wife will have!"

"I don't think so," he said. "Although, to be sure, the lot of a country doctor's wife is not cast in velvet ease."

"A country doctor! Are you going to persist in that? I can't talk you out of it?"

"Why should you?"

"But why?" exclaimed Luisa. "I mean—that is—I know it is no affair of mine!"

"I did have other views——"

"Of course you did. Why, just think what you could do at the bar! And you would be in politics——"

"Politics!"

"Yes, indeed; you would be senator; you would——"

"No. I wished to study for the ministry."

"Oh!" and she struck a spark of fire from two flints in her hand, and then tossed them away.

"And my mother wished it, too," said John, unobservantly. "But my father thought otherwise. He thinks I am adapted for his work. And he says it is the Master's work. And when my mother remembers what it has done for my father, she says she cannot ask more for me, and there you have it," he added, seating himself on an edge of the bowlder behind her. "And so I am studying with him for the present. But I shall go down to the medical school, as I told you, and after that, perhaps again across the water for Vienna, and to walk the Dublin Hospital——"

"To come back and practise up here among the hills! But to be sure. What am I thinking of?" opening her eyes. "You will be a great city physician. You will be the fashion. You will have an income of forty thousand a year!"

"There is quite as much to do here among the hills."

"You don't mean to say you would really settle here? To take care of boors and bumpkins? To waste yourself on clods?"

"There is no such thing as waste, you know—see that rainbow! And as for that, my father is a country doctor."

"I should think it was enough, then, to have one such power thrown away."

"We don't look at it so. There are bodies and souls of value here. My father thought it worth while, when Mr. Morris died, to bring here a preacher of as rare gifts as there was to be had——"

"Yes, I know. Mary told me herself.

And he pays him out of his own pocket a big salary. She told me not to speak of it. But then, of course, you knew."

"No, I didn't. And, excuse me———"

"I should have minded Mary, and my own business," said Luisa, laughing. "I was never taken up so shortly and so frequently in my life. There is something in the atmosphere of these hills very conducive to frankness."

"I beg your pardon."

"No, indeed. But you see my excuse is that you are all so different here, and you interest me."

"Thanks," said the young man.

"And now you are offended. But you are—like the people in a book. Mary is so white and fair and Blessed Damozel seeming. St. Paul or St. John, or some of them, Luke, perhaps, would have looked exactly like the doctor. And as for your mother — those old Hebrews and Arabs didn't think much of women, did they! or there would have been a seraph of their naming to compare your mother with! Oh —and, of course," she cried, "I've made another blunder now! You call it playing with sacred things."

"If you say nothing worse than that," said he, "I fancy you will be forgiven." And the smile that played round his lips and kindled the rather severe outlines, as he looked down at her, who gazed up at him with the light sparkling in her gypsy-like eyes, and the color glowing in her velvet cheek, was all that was needed to send the dimples dancing over Luisa's face again.

"Well," she said, "when I see you galloping by as if you had a lariat coiled on the saddle-bow, I must say you don't look as if the future of a country parson or a country doctor was the one you had chosen for yourself!"

"I really don't know why either of those people should not ride a good horse."

"All the same, I believe. I shall go into Tucson, or another such spot, some day yet, and see you with a cowboy's hat and cartridge-belt, speaking with your gun for all it's worth."

" May your prophetic powers increase."

" I suppose you mean to say they never can be less.   Well, Mary ought to be tired holding the horses," she said.   " And I'm sure I'm tired.   Hills are all very well to look at.   But I never could live on scenery. I want people, too, and all the touch and go of life.   I can't have the go without the touch.   And yet, who knows ? " she said. " I think if I lived long among such people as you are here, I might be—in time—just a fraction as good.   What they call not half bad, you know."   And she lifted her hand for him to help her up and forfend her in the scramble down to the hollow, where Mary had waited with the horses.

" Oh, I rode all one fall with the Myopias," said Luisa, as they mounted and went on, " but it was nothing like this !   I feel every instant as if I were going to slip over the edge of the earth.   Mary, what possesses you to sit up in your saddle that

way? You ride like one of the Wild
Ladies!" And John had to dismount and
give Mary his bridle-rein, and lead Luisa's
horse himself, to the accompaniment of
shrieks and laughter and blushes and great
gayety. And it was early dusk when they
reached the village and found Miss Barbara
at the Camperdoun gate with old Martha,
just properly disquieted and no more.

"Oh, no," said Miss Barbara, with sus-
picious sweetness, "I felt you must be perfectly safe with Mr. John. He knows every
cleft of the hills, Martha says. Thanks!
Thanks!" to the young man. "Good-
night! Good-night!" and she turned with
her charge.

"Well, I hope, Luisa," she added, after
the door was closed, "you are not going to
treat this one as you have treated all the
young men at home—let him get interested
in you and then drop him——"

"Into nether blackness," said the girl.
"Aunt Barbara, I should think you considered me a perfectly hopeless flirt."

"I do," said Miss Barbara.

They went in and sat in the old parlor, just where the light of the hall lamp fell on the portrait of the girl that Luisa used to say would drive her wild if she met her in the dark.

"If these people weren't crazy," she said, expecting some expostulation, and thinking to ward it off, "they got themselves up for the part. They'll drive me crazy some dark night yet. Aunt Barbara, we must put some netting over them, and have it thick——"

"When I came up here," said Miss Barbara, paying no attention to the new issue, "it was to arrange a matter of property. And I brought you along to be rid of love-making, not to plunge into more. And as for this young man, Luisa, he is the only child of his father and mother, and I can't have you playing with him."

"I am not playing with him," said Luisa.

"I don't dispute that he is, all things

considered, eligible. Yes, eligible, and pre-
sentable—an only son, idolized. Dr. Donner, I understand, is a very wealthy man
now, and with a large income besides from
mica mines and wood-lots and what not.
And money grows—there's no doubt of
that. And if you are in earnest about
young John Donner," said Miss Barbara
slowly, " and if he chooses to come down
and settle in town, we could soon fetch him
a practice. He has seen the world ; is col-
lege-bred ; is serious—it would give you
stability ; yes, indeed, I think well of it."

"Aunt Barbara !" shrieked Luisa, from
the lounge, "what in the world are you
talking about ? You are all out. You are
just as much mistaken as if you had torn
your gown. My goodness ! what do I want
of him ? He is dead in love with Mary."

"So was *Romeo* with *Rosaline.* It was
before he had seen you. ' When I said I
would die a bachelor I did not think I
should live till I were married,' said *Bene-
dick.* He isn't dead in love with Mary

now." And at that Luisa caught up her
hat in a fine temper and rushed to her room
and locked the door, and flung herself on
her bed in a passion of tears.

"Oh!" she sobbed, "I don't care a
scrap! And I know he doesn't care a scrap.
He is in love with Mary; he ought to be,
I want him to be! Oh, to think I've only
been here six weeks, and am in all this
trouble! Oh, what was I born for? I will
go home; I will go right home; the house
is there whether the family is or not.
And oh, I don't know! I don't know—
how I—can—go away!" And then she
pulled the other pillow over her head in a
whirl of pride and shame—the handsome,
haughty Luisa, who had been so long in the
habit of breaking hearts with her black eyes
and her damask cheeks and her bewildering
smiles and her silver voice, that she never
knew she had a heart of her own to break!

And while Luisa was crying in her pillow,
and rising and walking the floor, and bath-
ing her eyes, and beginning to cry again,

Mary leaned over the gate with John and watched the moon float up full over the crest of Benbow, and John watched its silver glorying of her face and her fair hair and her great night-blue eyes.

"I am so sorry," she was saying, "that I was born anywhere but here. I love it all so. I should like to feel I was its very own."

"You would not advise me, then, to go down and open my practice in the city?" he asked after a moment.

"I? Oh, John, never! To be sure," she added, with rather a regretful intonation, "you might become more famous there; have more opportunity——"

"There is all the opportunity in the world here," he said, quickly. "And I must be with my father."

She turned in a little surprise, as if she saw he had been weighing a point about which there was no question. The minister, who had no more wisdom, despite his gifts, than to step down just then and join them, thought he had never seen anything so beautiful as his daughter standing there in the moonlight like a statue that has just melted into a woman. Perhaps John thought so, too. But as he gazed, a thin cloud drifted across the moon, and in the place of that innocent white still beauty swam a little dark face, all blush and smile and sparkle, glancing, laughing, flashing, living, and dazzled and dimmed his eyes.

But old Martha was, on the whole, something wiser than the minister. She had seen John dashing off the next morning, in his saddle, for a long ride up and down hill. "Ye needn't go horseback riding," she muttered to herself, although apparently addressing him as he galloped by, "to work it off. It's only time cools hot blood—an' ye come rightly by it! But ye're yer mother's son, ez well ez his'n, an' ye've got the stuff in ye ter overcome ten'tation. Ye've got princerple, John Donner! An' ef this little minx o' ourn ain't tew much fer ye, ye'll clap it right on now!"

Apparently John had no sympathetic way of taking the unheard advice to heart, for he came up the yard the evening of that day, scattering with his stick the petals of the poppies by the path.

But before he could drop the knocker, Martha, who had been on the watch, came out and closed the door behind her.

"She's ben to bed all day 'ith the headache, an' you can't see her," she said. "An' ez for you, John Donner, you jes' put me in min' of a fly 't can't keep away frum the honey, pizon in it or not! I've hearn tell of men 't was in love 'ith two women ter oncet, but I didn' expec' ter see 'em in a Christian lan'. Now, you better go home tell ye know yer own mind. What! Oh, ye ain't no need to look glowering to me! I ain't a gal, an' I don't mind yer looks the leastestest mite. Ye'd be ez harnsome as the Archangel Gabriel—as ye be—an' I shouldn't see it, an' ye can stan' up as big an' forbiddin' as Mount Pisgeh, an' I shouldn't be afraid of ye. I should only see

the little boy thet uster run acrosst the green
ter old Marthy fer her hot gingerbread.
Wal', I'm takin' better care o' my hot
gingerbread now——"

"What in the world are you talking
about, Aunt Martha?" said the young
man, impatiently, looking up at the house.

But Martha took a step nearer, and laid
her old seamy hand on his arm. "Now,
John," said she. "I give ye the fust kiss ye
ever hed—yes, I did! I was yer mother's
nuss. Mr. Camperdoun, he lent me—an'
I'd 'a' gone ef he hedn't. An' I've ben
fond o' ye sence ye were so high. An' I've
watched out on ye, an' prayed for ye, an'
ben proud of ye."

"Yes, Aunt Martha, I know it," said the
young man. "And I recognize and return
all your friendship. I don't know just what
you are driving at now."

"Yes, ye do. I ain't ben all the same's
own folks to ye all yer life fer nothin', an'
ye know me well enough ter know w'at I
mean. 'Cause I'm fond o' you ain't the

reason I'm willin' ter see ye go straight ter destruction."

" Well, look here," said the young man, laughing now, " if this is all you have to say——"

" 'Tisn't. An' you needn't laugh. On-less you want ter laugh t'other side yer mouth. 'Tain't no laughin' matter. Fond ez I be of you, John Donner, I've ben jes' ez fond o' Mary Swann, ever sence she lighted in this town like a little white bird. It seemed ez ef she was too good ter stay, an' I vum I do'no' but she be ! She's a sight too good fer ye, anyway, playin' fast an' loose ez ye be. Now, maybe," said Martha, with half a wheedling emphasis " you ain't jes' so's ter say engaged to Mary, but ye know ye ain't eyther of ye expected ter marry anybody else. Ye know she's cut out for ye, an' there ain't nobody else in this breathin' world that's fit ter be yer blessed mother's darter, an' 'twould nigh about break her heart to hev Mary's heart broke."

"Come, come, Aunt Martha," said the
young man, "you will have to let me pass."

"W'en I'm ready. I ain't said my say
yet. I'm yer mother's an' yer father's
friend. I knowed 'em afore ye did. An'
that's one side of it. The other is," and
Martha's little pale eyes flashed at him,
"I've been hired help in the Camperdoun
fambly this thirty year come nex' month.
Their fortins hes ben mine. I've ben true
to 'em, an' I mean ter be. Where the
Camperdouns is consarned, I'm a Camperdoun," and there Martha choked a little,
but not at all with any fear of the disdain
of the landed gentry among whom she had
taken her place, and reached up and pulled
the comb out of her hair and gave the gray
wisp a stronger twist, as if the tension
tightened her control over her feelings.
"An' so ye see," she began again, after
thrusting in the comb more firmly, "I can't
hev no playin' 'ith this here little minx.
She may be a poppet," said Martha, "but
she's a Camperdoun. An' she's a dear,

pooty, coaxin' little cat, an' I'm fond o'
her, tew. An' that's all they is about it.
An' I tell ye, ef ye don't let her alone, John
Donner, I'll go to yer father. An' then we'll
see. Hev ye forgot," she exclaimed, her
voice rising, " that she's got w'at yer father
calls the Camperdoun inheritance, jes' ez
much ez the worst of 'em ? Don't ye know
this girl's got the thing in her blood, jest
ez strong ez Launce Camperdoun hed, ef
there's anythin' wakes the sleepin' beast ?
Ef that there Miss Barb'ry's name warn't
Camperdoun I wouldn't hev one mite o'
respec' for her," cried the old woman, with
fervid inconsequence. " Fer ef I know
black an' w'ite w'en I see it, it was her give
him his death notice w'en she sent him
word they was cousins, and 'twarn't no use
doublin' crazy blood, or words to that ef-
fec'. I come an' nussed him through brain-
fever, an' arter that he jes' wilted down. I
s'pose she done right, though. In the end,
that is. But she'd orter thought o' thet in
the uptake. An' ye see that ye do right,

John Donner! I won't hev this Loizy o'
ourn tampered with. Let sleepin' dogs lie.
She'll do well enough ef thar don't nothin'
pertic'lar come acrost her hawse, ez they say.
But she sha'n't be upset by a feller thinkin'
he's in love with her w'en he knows in his
soul he's agoin' ter marry another gal."

A blind slammed open on the second
floor, a head where the sunset glinted in
points of light on every dark ring of hair
was thrust through the open window, a
laughing face looked down at him. "I've
had a headache," said Luisa. "I'm all
right now. Stay a moment. I'll be down
directly."

Mary waited, leaning on the garden-gate
alone that night, and went in when the nine-
o'clock bell rung, with a sort of chill at her
heart that she had never felt before. She
didn't know why it was that, as she copied
out her father's sermon for him the next
day, she listened for a sound the morning
long with a painful eagerness ; the sound of
a familiar foot on the gravel that did not

come ; and that when she put the little children to bed for her mother, and sat singing
to them in the twilight, the beating of her
heart made her voice tremble so that the
boy reached from his bed and put an arm
about her neck and whispered, " Buvver
loves Mawy."

Buvver was ill next day, and when Luisa
ran down for Mary to join them on a tramp
up the Weathergauge, Buvver would not
hear of Mary's leaving him ; and, of course,
Mary would not cross the sick child's whim,
and she stayed at home, but with the heart
going out of her and up the mountain-side
where the party scrambled. She contented
herself as she could by thinking of the high
pasture where she and John had sat while
the sun revealed the mysteries in the front
of old Blue opposite, the long descending
slope between peopled with the wild horses
of the doctor's upper farm, and Blue Mountain rising with layers and lines of pine
forest, into which presently wound veils of
smoke, while the forest as it climbed became

deep violet glooms suddenly smitten and
parted by rifts of sunshine, disclosing, still
above, bare, scarred precipice and leaping
torrent and misty caverns; and the heights
beyond, swathed in deep, impenetrable
azure, seemed, she had said to John, to be
both the throne and the high altar of Power.
She wondered if John would not remember
her there.   And as she sat beside the bed
where Buvver was now asleep she was
ashamed of herself that her breath went and
came so eagerly; that she found it so hard
to sit still; that the unreasonable tears
would start and drop upon her work.

Perhaps John would have remembered
her there, if he had gone there—for the unspoken words that had trembled on his lips
as they had rested there were like those
strains that " pipe to the spirit ditties of no
tone," and they had both known what the
presence of others hindered from further
expression.   But to-day the party wound
round the Weathergauge by another path;
and after luncheon he had been sitting with

Luisa, a little apart from the rest, looking at quite a different view—the view of a rosy face where dimple chased dimple, where white eyelids drooped their dark lashes over dark eyes and lifted them with flashes of laughing light, and little teeth glittered, and the corners of a pretty mouth curved bewilderingly; the face of a woman like those he had read of, a woman of the great outer world with its dash and life and sparkle, such as he had seen but not approached in Paris perhaps; a woman fit for the life of courts, and smiling now on him. And they had risen and strolled away, following a track John knew, now under arches of green boughs where he had to clear the tangle; now pausing to look at the world through open spaces while they discussed their young experiences and opinions; now resting before starting to go down and find the others; and at last wrapped in a cloud that came up about them and played its lightnings to and fro under their feet.

" I think we will climb a little higher and get out of these mists," said John. " And if we keep to the left there's a path down. I have heard my mother say that when it is dark where we are it is best to climb higher and into the light."

" That is one of the good things," said Luisa, with a little sigh. " It isn't my way. I should just shut my eyes and fight on."

" There isn't much fighting here," said John.

" No ; only marching and countermarching. And I have my marching orders. I shall be going home so soon now," she said, with another little sigh.

" Going home ! " And he stood still with sudden consternation.

" Yes. They are all settled on the Shore by this."

" I thought—I hoped——"

" Oh, Aunt Barbara is going to stay," said Luisa, demurely.

" What in the name of wonder——"

" Do you care whether Aunt Barbara

stays or not, I suppose you want to say. Well, she will have the place ready for the family by another season.''

''Another season. It might as well be another life.''

''Exactly,'' said Luisa. And then she stopped and looked behind her. ''I thought the others would be somewhere here,'' she said. ''Oughtn't we to go back? Sha'n't we lose them?''

''What do we want of the others?'' he asked, roughly.

She shrugged her shoulders.

''You said there were no bears in these woods,'' she said, with a side glance.

He laughed then. ''You make no allowances,'' he began.

''What nonsense!'' interrupted Miss Luisa.

''To be sure, it is impossible for you to see, to know—I don't imagine a rose blowing all alone would have any idea of what the world would be without it.''

''I'm sure I don't know how roses feel.

I hardly think science has gone so far. Though I always did believe flowers felt it when you picked them. But just now," she exclaimed, coming to a halt, "have you really any idea where we are? It doesn't seem to me that this is even a bridle-path. Chaperones do have their uses, don't they? If there were such things at Woodsedge, we—could have lost ourselves on Weathergauge just the same."

John started and looked about him.

"I thought I knew every twig on the Weathergauge," he replied. "We—we really must wait where we are till the sky lifts." And he began to break off some hemlock boughs for her to sit upon.

As she waited, watching his movements, something of her thought concerning his splendid young stature and strength shot so swiftly into her face that he cast down his eyes.

"Yes," he exclaimed, suddenly, "the first man might have been breaking boughs for the first woman, as I am doing——"

"But she wouldn't have worn a bicycle suit from Ballard's," said Luisa. "Why are you cutting so many boughs?"

"It may come up cold," looking away after a quick glance. "I may have to cover you, while I go up on the ledge and build a fire to tell them where we are."

"You don't mean to say—how romantic! How Penny Gower would enjoy this! Are we really lost?"

"Not exactly," he said, piling the plumy boughs. "There," he continued, seating her on the soft, fragrant heap, and throwing himself down beside her. "When the sun sets I think it will open the clouds below, and we shall see our way. There is nothing to be afraid of. I have an idea," he said, "that we have wound round the mountain, and that the shaking heath is some hundreds of feet below us. That shaking heath is like a piece of the Debatable Land. The common people used to declare it was possessed by spirits, for it is ubiquitous; a piece of it comes almost into town, and it encircles the base of Weathergauge ten miles away, except for the causeway by which we crossed. I suppose Weathergauge was some old volcano, rising from the lake once."

"Adam and Eve and the beginning of the world," said Luisa. "Quite genealogical."

It grew dusky, and the wind, sweeping by, freshened.

"Do you know," she said at last, looking up gravely, "if we only were lost, and were never to be found, and it were the real end of all things here for us——"

She stopped, her voice trembling. He took her hand and kept it; it fluttered a moment like a bird, and then lay still in his. She was so near that her breath fanned warm on his cheek.

"There is no such fortune," he said, "good or bad. And I—had rather live with you, than die with you!" And the next moment his arms were about her and he had kissed her on the mouth.

They neither of them spoke for a long while. The moment was enough; alone, above the world, in each other's arms! They had no idea if it were a moment or an hour that they lingered, with murmurs, with caresses, with simple silence of rapture. There is nothing by which to measure time in Paradise. And then it began to grow light about them, and out of a great golden glamour the friendly face of the moon looked through.

"Oh!" cried Luisa, "that is the end. There is the light and the world and life again!"

"This is life," said John. "And there is the heath, as I thought. Now our way is clear and safe. My mother told me the happiest night of her life was on the edge of that heath, where once she was lost and had abandoned herself to the love and care of heaven, and my father came and found her and snatched her back to the love here. And here, just above, Luisa, has been and is the happiest night of my life, too."

And for answer, Luisa burst into tears, sobbing vehemently, uncontrollably.

"What is it? Oh, what is it?" cried John.

"Nothing, nothing!" she sobbed. "Only I have been so happy, and life is so short, and things—things are so cruel. Oh, how could Paolo and Francesca have been in hell when they were together!" And he held her, and she clung to him, till the tears stopped, and hand in hand, with whispered words of endearment, as if they feared the very trees should hear, they took their way down.

It was that forenoon that Mrs. Donner had come across the green to Mary.

"Buvver is better," she said. "Nothing really ailed him, the doctor says. He does not need you, indeed, dear soul, and I do. Your mother is willing, Maida is packing your trunk, and we are going on a little journey together, you and I. The doctor thinks the salt air will be good for both of us. And he can't go; and I can't go alone, and you haven't seen the sea for years, Mary. John will come and bring us home, I hope. And there isn't a half hour to spare.''

An hour before that the doctor had said to his wife, as he saw the young people going by the gate with their baskets, and taking the Weathergauge lane, '' I suppose you haven't noticed Master John's fancy for the little Camperdoun puss ? ''

'' Yes, I have,'' she said, somewhat dejectedly. '' I am afraid I have. And I had so wished for something else, you know.''

'' You will have something else,'' he said, smiling at her, as she sat folding and unfolding the white Liberty scarf round her shoulders. '' It is only a fancy, an infatuation, if I know the signs. It will pass presently, like any phase of the moon. Yes, I have seen and heard too much of the Camperdoun taint to have my son's life ruined by it. While he is waiting for my consent he will outgrow it. This part of him is my son,'' he said, still looking at her and won-

dering, without knowing that he did so,
what further loveliness heaven could add
to her. "But if history repeats itself it is
on the upward spiral here. And I haven't
any fear for your son, my wife. He will
come out all right."

"It troubles me to think," she said,
"that he will make me his confidante when
he is ready. And it will be the first time
he has not had my sympathy."

"Then he shall not make you his confidante. It will be best for him not to do so.
To confide a thing is to cement it, in a way.
You shall go off somewhere. I suppose I
can live while you are gone. To come
home at night and not find you—it is a
sacrifice. Nancy, I never dreamed youth
would last so long. What is the rhyme the
children were saying, 'Monday's child is
fair in the face, Tuesday's child is full of
grace,'—you must have been born between
the two, for you are as fair to me to-
day——''

"There, there," she said, smiling, and

taking his knotty hand and passing it across her lips. "I was never fair, you know."

"The years have moulded your soul into your face!" he said. "Yes, I know how it will be; the moment you are gone I shall begin to quake lest it is a delusion that you care for your old man still."

"One would think it was a superior being. I am only your old wife."

"There is no wife so beautiful as an old wife."

"I hope John will think so when his time comes," as she laid her cheek upon the hand she still held.

"Ah! John, yes—well," he paused a moment. "What do you say to the Shoals?" he asked then.

"It seems like running away in the face of danger."

"It is best for John. I might be able to run down by and by. And I think a little toning up with the open sea will do you no harm."

"I will take Mary with me," said Mrs. Donner.

And so it happened, as John wound down the mountains, threading the narrow greenwood ways, lifting the rain - drenched branches, scaring the wild bird from her nest, climbing round bowlders, and coming out of the shadow down the long wet pastures into the glory of the moonlight, his feet upon the earth, his head in a cloud of joy, that his mother and Mary were speeding away in a sleeping-car, with the iron echoes beating round them as they clanged along, like an everlasting resonance of bolts and chains shot home and barring them out of happiness.

But when there is a disturbance in the atmosphere for one or two people, there is apt to be at the same time a disturbance for several. As Miss Barbara Camperdoun at her door was surveying the clouds, just before the thunder-storm burst over the valley, she hardly saw the carriage taking Mrs. Donner to the station, for at the same moment she saw a figure strangely familiar coming along the dusty road—yellow umbrella and camp-stool and other fine artistic belongings under his arm, and a generally weary air about him, as he also looked at the clouds, not to be mistaken.

"My gracious!" she exclaimed, as she went in quickly and shut the door. "Was there ever anything more unfortunate? There isn't a moment to lose. I shall speak to Dr. Donner at once, and tell him what I propose to do for Luisa, if she marries to please me. And I really think she might go further and fare worse. He can't do less for John. He will do more. Yes, I think the house will be on the Avenue. But the nail must be clinched now, for Luisa's as changeable as the day. What in the name of goodness sent Penny Gower to Woodsedge now?"

V

THE thunder-storm that had swept through the valley while the party of young people rested on the ledges of Weathergauge had left the air next morning more light and nimble than that round *Macbeth's* castle, and Miss Barbara Camperdoun had recovered from the fright into which thunder always cast her, sufficiently to remember the look on Luisa's face as John had parted from her at the gate, and she had darted past her aunt and old Martha and up to her own room, something disordered, something flushed—Miss Barbara could not tell if that look were one of purpose, of joy, or of agony.

" It is all settled ! " said Miss Barbara to herself. " And, of course, it has excited her. She is such a little free and independent spirit, she does not take kindly to the idea of being mastered, and it is plain that love has mastered her at last. Well,

I'm glad things have declared themselves before Penny Gower, with his ridiculous attractions, came upon the scene to make a diversion. And as I said this noon, the very first thing I'll do to-morrow is to see Dr. Donner and have the thing made irrevocable. With what the doctor is able to allow, and I am convinced that is something extraordinarily handsome, and with what I can do," said Miss Barbara, counting off imaginary sums on her fingers, " few young people have a better start in life than they will have. Yes, it is decidedly the best chance Luisa has had, or is likely to have. I'm sure I don't know who there is—and I want her settled! We will get him a Back Bay practice, with the kind of people that go out of town from May to October, so that they can come up here for four months in the year at least. And the more I see of this ideal village and this ancestral place of ours, the more fit I think it all is! And, for my part, I shall have a load off my mind when Luisa is married and tied down to some duties, for I never know what in the world the little brimstone is going to do next! It certainly is a misfortune to be an only daughter and a beauty, and have a spirit and a will, and lovers, and all that. Dear, dear me, it is nearly midnight now! I wonder if they have such storms here frequently— thunder does always string me up so!''

So it was early in the morning when a note, written in Miss Barbara's most mannish hand, but sealed with her most ladylike wax, and asking his presence for a brief interview, was put into Dr. Donner's hand.

The doctor was breakfasting by himself, and feeling exceedingly lonesome. He missed the face opposite him for so many mornings of so many years—for even when his wife had been up all night with the sick she had always made shift to pour his coffee; and he felt as if there were something gone wrong in the relation of things without it — the face that might be old and plain, but in which the sweetness of the spirit, as he had told her, had wrought a loveliness that to

him was more than beauty, and that of late
years it had never crossed his mind to doubt
was beautiful to all the world besides. He
was thinking of her as he slowly sipped his
coffee. A bitterness of sudden remembrance of those early days, and what now
seemed to him her divine patience in endur-
ing them, made even his cup taste bitter.
He thanked heaven, as he bent his head in
the silent grace, that she had never known
his baseness in marrying her as he did. He
felt as he thought of it afterward while fill-
ing his phials that he could not have borne
her righteous contempt. He felt, too, that
he could even less well have borne the sting
of anguish it would have been to her. He
thanked heaven for another thing—as in his
practice he had noticed that the son, although he might have the father's physical
resemblance, was almost invariably the
moral and mental and spiritual child of his
mother—that John was his mother's son;
and as he thought of it, John seemed to him
to have an immense advantage, a tremen-

dous spring-board for his work in the fact
that he was his mother's son. It was already a consecration for the Master's work.
" And there is need of him," thought the
doctor. " Here, it may be, too. For
where there was one Break o' Day with all
its miseries, one Dawlish's when I was a
lad, there are five now—farther off, to be
sure," for neither of those places existed
now in Woodsedge, " but still within reach,
and fermenting evil, needing the strength of
his mighty young frame and the purity of
his principle." And then it flashed over
him, not for the first time, the conviction of
the boy's feeling if he knew of the early life
of his father. And he groaned in spirit.
" Well, well," he said. " We are forgiven
a sin when we have reached a point where
we could by no possibility commit it again.
And if I have the Lord's forgiveness, I
think I must rely on the boy's. And in all
probability he will never have a dream of it.
For who would have the temerity to speak
of it to him ?—there is not a creature in the

world so cruel, so ignoble. Come, come, this is a poor beginning of a day's work! And the young fellow on his horse half-way up Weathergauge already—I wish he hadn't to have this pain that I fear may be coming —but it would be worse pain by and by. Somehow the best we have comes through pain. His mother will make it all right, though.'' As he went out, he saw lying on the table in the hall the white Liberty scarf that his wife had worn the day before; he took it up and kissed it; it had lain in one of her old sandal-wood boxes, and carried the delicate scent, sweet and evanescent, that was always about her garments, and he put it in his breast-pocket before reading the note from Miss Barbara that Sally handed him.

It was but a short distance across the green to the Camperdoun house under its great oak-trees. Not waiting for his gig, the doctor strolled over, his hands in his pockets, except when he took them out to put them on the curly heads of two children

running along on either side of him a little
way, Brow, the grandson of old Brow, following at his heels in the hope of a frolic
with Bursar, and he paused at the Camperdoun gate for a draught of the fresh, dewy
fragrance that blew down from the mountain-
side and curled about the valley, and seemed
to fill it with strength and courage, and all
the deliciousness of life besides. The doctor had need of that long draught of brac-
ing air and vigor before he turned and went
up the path to meet Miss Barbara at the
door.

She took him into the west parlor, a cool
and shadowy place in the morning, with its
heavy damask curtains, whose moss-green
hues had long since faded to a silver-olive
sheen, and among whose old spider-legged
mahogany and dark imprisoning portraits
Launce Camperdoun had been wont to
spend his sunsets and long evenings. It
was all the same as it had been, except for
the great jars of fresh flowers that stood
about here and there. But it gave Dr.

Donner a more than passing mood of sad-
ness to recall the life that had been lived
and had gone out here in its mild mad-
ness; and as he stood looking at the picture of Camperdoun in his youth, in the
niche over the fireplace, he found tears in
his eyes.

Luisa had not yet come down; the little
maid who helped Martha had been told to
bring her toast and tea to her room some
time ago. So Miss Barbara felt herself at
perfect liberty. Not that she anticipated
any difficulty—of course she was doing the
Donners an honor which they would recognize and acknowledge; but still she pre-
ferred to have the doctor by himself.

"Pray be seated, doctor," she said.
And she could not have told you why she
felt a slight sensation of awe, as if in the
presence of majesty, when this man, who
used to break her uncle's horses, took the
great arm-chair near her own and laid his
arm along the ebony table there.

"I hope you are not very much occupied

this morning," she said, blandly; "for I want your counsel and agreement concerning our young people."

"Our young people?" inquired Dr. Donner.

"Yes—Luisa and your son. They are—as, to be sure, you are aware—very much —interested, I may say, in each other," said Miss Barbara, hesitating a little at the calm unsuspiciousness of the doctor. "I had supposed they had a warm mutual interest," she said, hurriedly, "and with very good reason. And I had thought of bringing the affair to your attention before. But last night when they came down from the mountain—Weathergauge, do you call it? —I was quite sure from Luisa's face that they had arrived at a happy understanding——"

"I hope not," said the doctor, gravely.

"You hope not?"

"I mean that with every wish for their happiness—so much so, indeed, that it is absurd to speak of it," said the doctor, "yet anything such as you imply would be very unfortunate."

"Very unfortunate?"

"I think so."

"Not at all," said Miss Barbara, re-mounting the heights from which she had been startled. "Not at all, when it is with my full approval."

"What," began the doctor, in his deepest tones, "what——"

"Has that to do with it?" said Miss Barbara, so affable and sprightly that she was half astonished at herself. "Why, everything!"

"I really fail to see——"

"I hardly expected you would. And of course I am conscious that, looking at it from the point of view of the last generation," said Miss Barbara, with much sweet condescension, "something might be said about a misalliance. But we are living in this generation. And you have become so eminent in your profession, Dr. Donner, and have accumulated such wealth——"

"Who knows anything about my wealth?"
said the doctor, stoutly.

"And John being your only child,"
continued Miss Barbara, not allowing herself to falter, although feeling the ground
less firm beneath her feet, "that—why, all
that puts a very different face upon the affair."

"Miss Barbara," said the doctor, more
gently, "wiser people than we have made
mistakes——"

"Oh, no, indeed, not in the least!" she
exclaimed with assurance. "There is no
mistake about it! I have not lived in the
world of men and women for nearly sixty
years not to know love, and first love, *par
parenthèse*, when I see it. Trust a woman
for that! Luisa is a girl of strong feelings,
and no one of her lovers has ever touched
them before. I must admit that there is
something — something — very compelling
about this young man — his face, his figure,
his manner — and then, brought up as he
has been, his mother's companion——"

The doctor bowed.

"Ah! I thought you would see it as I do——"

"By no means," said the doctor. "This is all a mistake, Miss Barbara, as I said before——"

"And as I said before, there is no mistake about it!" exclaimed Miss Barbara. "My niece, who is a belle and a beauty, and your son, who has a future before him, have chosen each other, for better, for worse."

"It would be decidedly for worse if they had done so," said the doctor, moving his fingers impatiently on the table.

"I don't know what you mean!" cried Miss Barbara. "What insufferable breeding the man has!" she thought. "Drumming his fingers! And really it is quite too much mock humility. Of course, it's a great thing for his son — but he needn't pretend to misunderstand me so altogether abjectly!"

She used her smelling-salts a moment.

"I am told," she said then, "that your son is to follow your profession. With our family connection and friends, it will be easy to build up for him a good Back Bay practice very rapidly. With his talents he will soon make it a fine one. The Back Bay in Boston affords opportunities——"

"My son will practise his profession in and about Woodsedge," said Dr. Donner.

"Oh, I know you would not like to part with him—a son like that! But you would not have to do it. For at least four months of every year he would return, if he chose, and you and his mother would have him here. I should surrender to Luisa all my right and title to this house for their summer home, and to the whole of my cousin's property, indeed, as well as to some other—a few thousands, but enough to keep the wolf from the door," said Miss Barbara, with a genial laugh. "There will be something handsome, too, for Luisa on her father's death, but *festina lente*, we will not count on such contingencies," she said, gayly. "You, of course, are able to do much more on your side of the bargain—such are the *revanches* of fate—but, of course, Luisa's family and social relations count for a good deal." Miss Barbara had never been troubled by too much delicacy in her life. "Excuse me," she said, however. "It is not a time for sensitiveness in the weighing of advantages, and we are all going to be one family so soon it hardly signifies. And so," said Miss Barbara, "I sent for you this morning, Dr. Donner, to ask what settlement you would be willing to make on the young couple. I suppose Commonwealth Avenue would be the best, but a house on the water side of Beacon Street, between Berkeley and Exeter, has much in its favor. And there should be a certain yearly allowance to keep it up, of course, as Luisa's dress and her brougham and coachman would probably absorb the greater part of her own income, and she would be providing the house up here——"

"Miss Barbara!" exclaimed the doctor,

as soon as he had the chance, raising his
voice the least in the world, " you are going
altogether too fast. Allow me the opportunity of saying that I should give nothing to
my son in such an event. Nothing at all.
Not even my consent."

Miss Barbara looked at him with a puzzled,
almost a bewildered, air. " You would give
nothing—in such an event—not even consent," she repeated. " I—I don't think I
understand you."

" It is very simple," he said. " I tried
to spare you, Miss Camperdoun, when I
divined the drift of your thought——"

" You—spare—me ! " cried my Lady Disdain. " What in the world do you mean?"

" That I am unwilling to countenance
any such agreement as that you mention,"
he said, looking at her steadily. " And
for reasons of which you must be perfectly
well aware."

The sun fell on Miss Barbara's face, and
he rose to adjust the curtain, giving a nod
and smile as he did so to the pretty creature

standing by the althea-bush in the yard with
a young man beside her there—Luisa, who
had come down and was amusing herself
with Penny Gower.

"Do I comprehend you?" said Miss
Barbara. "Is it possible? Are you de-
clining for your son an alliance with my
brother's daughter?"

"She is a charming child, a lovely girl,"
said the doctor. "I could take her delight-
edly for my daughter, but not for my son's
wife."

Miss Barbara waited a moment, looking
at the table, and beginning to draw figures
there with the blunt point of a paper-knife.
It was very annoying. But then for Luisa's
sake—some diplomacy. "For what reasons?" she said, leaning forward, a little
breathlessly.

The doctor looked up; his eye swept, one
after another, the old portraits. He moved
his hand with a slight, quick motion toward
them. "The best of reasons," he said.
"There they are. I cannot—you must for-

give me—I cannot give my son any share in the Camperdoun inheritance."

"Speak more plainly!" commanded Miss Barbara, with flashing eyes.

"There is no need of that," he replied. "You know very well the traditions concerning every pictured person in this room, from your cousin Launce up. Is there one of them who did not suffer from the family taint?"

She waited a moment.

"I cannot believe," she said then, throwing down the ivory plaything, "that a man of your scientific acquirements can attach any importance to those old notions of heredity."

"I attach importance," he said, angrily at last in his turn, "to the Camperdoun insanity, which has gone from mother to son, and from father to daughter, for a hundred and fifty years, and I will not have my son made its victim."

"But they love each other," said Miss Barbara.

"They think they do, possibly. Two months ago my son was of a different opinion," said the doctor, a light shooting across the steel-blue eyes. "Your pretty Luisa came, a charming novelty—very like he swerved aside. I regret that he could be swayed—but it is pardonable. When she is gone, the fascination will be gone, too, and he will marry and be happy with the lovely girl who is fitted for him, has grown up with him, has my heart and his mother's, as well as his own—yes, under this infatuation, his own."

Miss Barbara was wondering at herself and her forbearance. Still, it might be worth while——

"But you really make too much of the matter," she said. "We do not regard it so seriously in society. A bar to marriage! At home one would be thought out of his head who entertained such an idea!"

"You entertained it once yourself, Miss Barbara."

"There were two of us," said Miss Barbara, with a slight start. "And really I don't know that it advances matters to use personalities."

"I beg your pardon; you have sought this interview and opened this conversation on nothing but personalities. You have compelled me to state plain facts and to use plain language."

And the doctor leaned back in his chair as if tired of the subject.

"Well, do you know," began Miss Barbara again, after another confidential moment with the paper-knife, "it seems to me you are fighting shadows. I think the trouble, such as it is, has died out."

"A thing never dies out by multiplying."

"But healthier blood—I will not say better blood—there is no better blood than the Camperdouns'!"

She paused; but the doctor said nothing.

"There has been only my cousin Launce of all this generation. For, of course, my brother's epileptic seizures——"

"Do not count, you would say. Excuse

me, they count for what they are worth. All insanity is not of the madhouse. Half the crimes of the world, and most of the crimes of what you call society, are but forms of insanity. Once the infection does its deadly work, those of the descendants who do not share its poison as madmen are the drunkards, the kleptomaniacs, the epileptics, the slaves of the senses, the women who abandon their children—— "

" How you talk ! That comes of living in the country with no companions but your own notions. I don't know anyone who would agree with you. Why, I won't say it is a patent of nobility, because I'm not claiming any merit on account of it, although it does imply a highly wrought and delicately sensitive organization, does it not? But upon my word, you won't find twenty families in our State, who think well of themselves—who have blue blood, you know— who haven't some member, near or far, in a retreat."

" My son's children," said Dr. Donner,

bending forward and gazing at her gravely, " will not be added to the number."

" Do you mean to say," cried Miss Barbara, all restraint giving way, "that you persist in such folly, that you are going to obstruct instead of assist this marriage? Do you know who you are, John Donner? Do you forget the time when you were my uncle's hired man——"

" I was hired to break your uncle's horses. I broke them well. I have never been afraid of wild rage in any form. I shall not sacrifice my son to it now," said the doctor, rising.

" Well," said Miss Barbara, " perhaps I ought not to have spoken exactly that way."

" Certainly you ought not ! " said the doctor, turning on her. " Your uncle was my benefactor. Your cousin was my friend. I, also, I was his friend. You should have remembered the long years in which I shielded him from himself and the world while he suffered under the black spell of his inheritance——"

She was not listening to him. Something had flashed across her recollection and was gone. What was this he said? He had been her cousin's friend. Of course he had! Why, there were those letters—there was that letter!

"Wait a moment!" she cried. "Wait a moment!" and she added to herself, "I have not done with you yet, Dr. Donner!"

She swept across the room to the old escritoire. The key stuck in the lock a second; she had time to reconsider, if she would. Reconsider! She had opened the matter out of pure goodness, she said to herself, as her thought flashed along the points. She remembered admiring John Donner, more than thirty years ago, as a splendid specimen of a man. She had thought now that an infusion of this strong blood into the tired Camperdoun race might be a good thing. She had been willing to overlook the social inequality. She had been very much afraid that Luisa would marry that Penny Gower, with nothing but his brush and palette to his name. She had always been afraid Luisa would do something eccentric, and she had thought that the sooner she should be tied fast in happy fetters, with husband and children, the better. She had, to be sure, been rather startled when she saw Luisa showing favor to young John Donner, and then she had thought, why not? "There is health, strength, virtue, wealth, all that is requisite —the very thing," she said. And she was fond of Luisa; the girl had always been her pet and darling; and now that her affections were engaged— Still, if the man here were going to oppose it, there was not much use in talking! Very likely that wife of his had her mind set on something else—Mary, the minister's daughter, of course. She would like to put a spoke in that wheel! And the man presuming to stand in her way —she a Camperdoun—he who had sprung from the clods of the valley! Miss Barbara's blood was up. There was nothing she had liked more than a fight all her life. She was not going under in this one, if she could help it, fair means or foul. Contest the point with her ! Decline an alliance with her niece ! He would, would he? "I will see about that ! " she said. It was not for Luisa now that she strove. It was not for love or happiness or anything of the sort. It was simply to carry her point, to overcome John Donner ! And her heart burned within her with revulsion from the certainty that he would accept her condescension, with anger that he should have dared oppose her, with determination to have her own way, now while she turned the key, took a bundle of papers from a pigeon-hole, fluttered her fingers to and fro among them and drew one out, and went back to the table where the doctor had again seated himself, and spread the yellow old sheet out before him.

" Do you remember that ? " she asked.

It was the letter in which he had announced his marriage to Launce Camperdoun. Dr. Donner arranged his glasses to look at it.

"If you do not withdraw all opposition and give your full consent and assistance to this marriage as I propose it," she said, "I will show this letter to your wife!"

As Dr. Donner began to read, it was with an entirely impersonal sense. Even his handwriting had changed so much in the course of years that he did not at first recognize this script as his own. And that life was so far away, he had so utterly and entirely outlived it, that it was a moment or two before he quite comprehended where he was.

"The cad!" he said, presently.

And then Miss Barbara's long, thin, yellow hand on the table, with its great emerald sparkling upon the lean, pointed finger that detained the sheet, caught his eye, and he saw that she was holding the sheet down to prevent his taking it; and the whole truth smote him that this shameful letter he had written himself, of his wife, and it was her purpose to let Nancy see it. He sprang to his feet with a cry. Nancy see this letter?

His face grew red as he thought of it—grew purple. He bent over the table, the veins all but bursting on his forehead, and the sweat beaded it in great drops. Not for all the wealth of all the Indies would he have Nancy see that letter! Not for the greatest joy of earth or the highest hope of heaven! Have Nancy know he was capable of such a villainy? There was a grossness of rascality in it that appalled him even now. To have Nancy know that he had been that dastardly wretch, to have her despise him—as she must—to have her loathe him? Oh, no! no! He put up his hands before his face, from which the color fled, and sat down and leaned back in the chair, white as the dead.

His pure-hearted, innocent Nancy! The beautiful soul, who believed in him so and —in all the pain he might have given her, he had given her, during those first years— had never known that he had not loved her, had never dreamed she had been subjected to such insult, such outrage! To have his dear wife so hurt, so irretrievably, so irreparably hurt—he cringed at the thought of the blow, the pain—and his the hand to deal it! His eyes as he looked up were like those of some great wounded wild creature, bloodshot, and full of anguish and bewildered imploring.

"Have you no mercy?" he stammered, with his stiff, white lips.

"Not the least particle," said Miss Barbara. "It isn't a case for mercy; it is a mere matter of business. You have to take care of your family. I am taking care of mine."

Through the open window came a pleasant hum of voices. It was Luisa, who knew she looked particularly well standing among the scarlet blossoms of the trumpet-flower trellis for Penny Gower to admire. They might have strolled away presently; it was as still outside as it was in the west parlor. The sound of the voices only made Miss Barbara set her teeth more firmly.

It was very warm. The doctor wiped his

forehead and tried to think again. The odor of the new lilies came curling into the room; the balsam-branch in the great fireplace oppressed him with its fragrance; he heard a cat-bird drop its shower of melody from the bough outside, and it struck him like a sound of pain; the murmur of the bees in the warm sunshine seemed to be buzzing in his brain. No, no, thrice no! He himself could endure the shattering of all his earthly happiness; he could endure anything, everything, but his wife should never have that cruel hurt, she should never know the dishonor she had suffered, she should never know there was a time he had not loved her.

Miss Barbara's long hand still lay across the paper, and her cruel, mocking eyes surveyed him.

"Well?" she demanded.

"You have no business with it," he said. "It is mine."

"No, it was my cousin's. He bequeathed me all he had. It is mine.

Simply as his executor it would be mine.
You can have it, though, on the conditions
named. What are you going to do about
it?''

His boy, then, was the price of that letter. He could save himself his wife's scorn,
he could save his wife the misery of that
knowledge—and that was the thing! He
could endure the scorn, but he could not endure her misery. It could all be spared by
giving his boy what was now the desire of
his heart, and would presently be fire under
his feet and ashes in his mouth. He could
save himself, he could save his wife, but
then the boy's life must be ruined. As he
sat there, that yellow sheet of paper seemed
to rise and hang in the air between him and
the sunshine. It was dark all around him;
he heard the rustling of the boughs sweeping
against one another in the soft summer wind
as if it were the murmur of another planet.
He fumbled for his handkerchief again, and
the Liberty scarf fell out, with its delicate
perfume, bringing his wife's presence almost

about him. Someone lifted a latch; he could not have told if the sound were leagues away or striking on his breast. But he stood up, supporting himself with both hands on the table, drenched to the skin and trembling. He knew what to do now.

He would not spare himself for the boy.

Neither would the mother spare herself for the boy.

It was all clear.

"Do as you please with the letter," he said. "But I will never give my consent to the ruin of my son by means of the Camperdoun inheritance."

At that moment the door that Miss Barbara had so carefully closed flashed open, and Luisa stood in the sunshine that burst through from the hall, as if she were radiant with it.

"I was under the window with Penny," she said, in a high, shrill tone. "Perhaps I have not heard all you have been saying, but I have heard enough! And that letter!

I don't know what is in it, but I know where it belongs!" and she snatched it from under her aunt's hands, tossed it on the balsam-boughs in the fireplace, and before Miss Barbara could hinder, scratched a match and sent bough and letter blazing and roaring up the big chimney.

Then she turned and faced the two again.

"You are quite right," she said to the doctor, her hands hanging before her, tightly clasped, and her face pallid. "I will not see your son again. I understand about the Camperdoun inheritance now. It is something not to be shared. I may never come to my own," she said, with a light and bitter laugh then, "but I will make no one else wretched with a peradventure. I will go down with Penny there and we will rub along——"

. "Penny!" shrieked Miss Barbara. "Are you mad already, Luisa! Marry Penny when——"

"Goodness gracious, Aunt Barbara!" said Luisa, in a perfectly matter-of-fact key. "You seem to think of nothing but marrying! I shall not marry anyone, now or ever. I shall not join the St. Margaret sisterhood, either," she added. "Helen Reynolds, Fanny Fairfield, and I are a sisterhood by ourselves. I shall just loiter along as I have been loitering, with Penny for a *pis aller*. He can't afford to marry. I can't afford to marry—with a difference. He will go on with his pictures that never sell. I shall go on with my flirtations that always sell."

The doctor looked up at her suddenly, as if roused from a stupor.

"No, no," she said, with a swift, deprecatory gesture. "I am all right. There is nothing the matter now. I am no more feather-brained than I always was. It hasn't broken out yet!"

"My dear child," said the doctor, tremulously, "it never may. In all probability it never will. Only, for my son's sake, I cannot accept the—the possibility."

"And I suppose you think I ought to

love God, who has given me such a horrible inheritance!"

"All the more, my poor little girl, you will have need of such a comfort and of its shield," he murmured, in a voice that sounded a long way off.

"I never knew about it," she said, wistfully, twisting a lock of her loosened hair, "till I heard Martha talking to him. And then I didn't wholly understand. And I didn't want to understand! I felt—I was sure—I knew it must all come to nothing. But I wanted to know what it was just to be—to be—oh, oh, so happy for one moment!" and she hid her face in her arms with a great sob.

"Luisa," said the doctor, trying to move toward her. And then his knees bent under him, he tottered and swayed, and slipped heavily to the floor.

Sitting by his father's side that night, holding his wrist, watching every pulse, every breath, John Donner read the note that Sally put into his hands, almost as un-comprehendingly as if it had been written to someone else, while the last echoes of the night - train went throbbing between the hills.

"It was all a mistake," the note ran. "Think of me as having been a little mad up there on Weathergauge, and forget me."

It dropped from his fingers as if it were a dead leaf, and seemed to have no more re-lation to him than if it had belonged to a previous life. All his being just then was centred in the beating of his father's heart, all his new skill was put to proof in keeping him alive, the physician from the other side of the hills having gone to lie down, and there was nothing in his consciousness but the love for his father, the fear for his mother.

The night had been hot; the windows were all wide open; the sunrise was in the room at last, luminous, purple, shot through and through with gold, and in the won-drous glow the great, dark peaks swam out

like giants couched about the bed and waiting on the sick man's breath. The rising
wind blew in a riot of fragrance and fresh-
ness, when the doctor opened his eyes and
lifted first one hand and then the other.

"Nothing but a vertigo," he said.
"Your mother must not know," and sank
away again.

And the weeks of effort, of suspense that
followed, with the endeavor to keep his
mother unaware, gave John so small time to
think of himself that when, in clearing off
some papers, he came across that little note
which cost Luisa such a heart-break, he was
aware only of a sense of relief.

He had a vague idea of what had happened. Had there been something wild
and wrong in his father's youth that his
mother was not to know? All the more he
loved him, and he held him in a passion of
tenderness. He would not let Martha or
Sally do a thing now that he could do himself, nor would he let the friends and country people who held their breath and would

gladly have risked their lives, perhaps have given them, for him who had been Providence to them, and had brought them and their dear ones up from the power of the grave.

At length then he took his father down, well again, if still weak, to his mother by the sea, having written to her constantly as if from his father too busy at first to write himself. At the last she had known something of the doctor's illness, but also that he was coming to her, and wished her to await him; and his wish had always been obeyed by her.

When the doctor waked in the late evening, in the soft, delicious dark, full of salt smells and of the wide singing of the sea, his head upon his wife's breast, her arms about him, "We are old people now," he said, "but, O my wife, not too old for love."

"With our whole heart!" she answered him.

" And are you sure I always loved you ? "

" Why, what ails you ? " she said. " You are weak. You are so tired," and she kissed his forehead and his mouth.

" And you forget the dark and evil days ? " he whispered.

" There never were any," she said. " The people offered thanks in all the churches of all the mountain-side for you, the day before yesterday, but I thank God for you every hour I live ! "

And while his father slipped back into purple dreams again, John was sitting high in a cleft above the sea with Mary, forefeeling the coming of the moon across the water, through the silvered dusk, watching some far-off, lonely breaker leap to catch the light, hearing the deep, melodious thunders plunge about them and fall away in stillness and come in again borne on the dripping winds from the midsea hollows. And when, in answer to his sigh, Mary laid her hand gently on his, he felt that there was health where she was, and that, at some time, life was going to be good again with this fair, white woman, whose beauty he could not see in the shadow. And his sigh was only for the sweetness of it all—the night, the sea, the returning love—the sigh of the finite in the presence of the Infinite.

www.ingramcontent.com/pod-product-compliance
Lightning Source LLC
Chambersburg PA
CBHW020005030726
47500CB00002B/449

9783743441781